This Little Pig

A Flak Anders Mystery
by

Lisa C Hannon

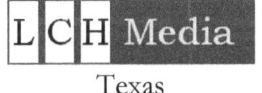

Texas

DEDICATION

Dedicated to Corey,
because he's everything;
and to Kelsey and John,
Tyler and Haley,
because they're everything else.

Thank you to
The DFW Writers' Workshop
and
the Fort Stockton Public Library's
Critique Café.

THIS LITTLE PIG

CHAPTER ONE

Sheriff Anita "Flak" Anders yanked the Crown Vic's steering wheel hard to the right, pulling the cruiser into the shallow ditch bordering the Appleby-Sand Road.

She wrenched the steering column gear shift up as far as it would go to put it in park, turned off the siren, but left the lights flashing, and radioed dispatch she was at the scene. A quick glance at the clock on the dash showed her it was nearly 2 a.m. She heard half of a crackly "10-4" as she got out of the car and slammed the door behind her.

The tanker fire engine blocked the dirt drive. She'd made good time—the firefighters unlimbered the hoses as she made her way past the truck. Rounding it, she spied the fire chief. He was easy to find in most situations at six foot six, but with boots and helmet on, he stood closer to seven feet tall. She walked up next to him and stood, arms folded, watching the activity. After a moment, she jogged him with her elbow. Due to the difference in their height, she caught him right about his hip bone, and rubbed her stinging elbow with her other hand. "Hey Garvey, what's the situation?"

He didn't even look down. "Hey, Flak. I told Dorrie to get you out here 'cause there's supposed to be somebody inside. It was too far gone to get my boys in—the roof had collapsed already by the time we got here. It's just a little old piece of crap house. Went up like dry brush."

Seemed to her like it was too fast. "Was it arson?"

"I don't know. How about letting us put it out first."

"I thought you might know already, since it went up like dry tinder." Flak moved a half step closer to Garvey to avoid the boys with the hoses.

"It's just a frame house, all wood and a tin roof. If the old man is in there, he's crispy by now."

"Who told you there was somebody in there?"

Garvey pointed to his right. Flak leaned in front of the big man to look where he indicated. A few yards away, a man in his mid-forties stood smoking a cigarette.

He was dressed only in a cowboy hat, shorts and boots. The swamp-like humidity of an East Texas summer combined with the heat of the fire covered every bit of his exposed skin with sweat, shining in the flickering light. The slow, rolling pain below her breastbone made it hard to catch her breath.

"Oh no." Flak straightened to keep Garvey's bulk between her and the other man, and concentrated on not putting her hand to her chest like some fluttering female.

Garvey's bass rumble came from high above her five-foot-four frame. "Yeah, I didn't think that'd make you too happy. How long y'all been divorced now?"

She pulled her shoulders back, moved her chin forward and blew a sigh upwards across her face to cool it some. "Well-l-l, we ain't exactly what you might call divorced."

"Dang, Flak, what's it been, three years? Four?"

"Something like that." It was four and a half actually, almost to the day.

"Well, that's y'all's business. But you might want to know he says that's his daddy going up in smoke." Garvey nodded his head toward the inferno.

"Crap, crap, crap." Flak reached up and settled her straw Stetson. "Well, I better get this over with." Circuiting around Garvey, she ambled over to the half-naked man grinding out a cigarette with the toe of his boot.

"Hey," was all she could come up with once she arrived. He had always left her tongue-tied, first out of love, and then out of anger, now—well, who knew? The effect he had on her was an eternal mystery to Flak.

He turned his head toward her, but the movement put his face in shadow, and obscured his expression. "Hey, Sheriff."

"Now, dang it, Curt." She swallowed the next words. Didn't seem like the right moment to be giving the man a hard time.

"Okay, then, Anita, what the hell do you want?" He bore down hard on the "hell," and made her given name sound like it tasted nasty. He turned his face to the fire.

"Garvey says your dad's in there."

"Yep."

"What makes you think so?" She tried hard to make the question inoffensive. She wasn't trying to make out he was lying, just figuring out what was going on.

"See that bicycle?" Curt pointed to the unmistakable two-wheeled frame, a dark shape against the side of the blazing building. "That's how he got around. If it's there, so's he."

The man's flat tones struck Flak as odd. "You don't seem very upset."

He lit another cigarette, not looking at her. "I don't know what I am right now."

She watched the tanker's crew flood the little dwelling and soak the pine trees that crowded in behind it. A burst of smoke followed the first loud, crackling hiss as water quenched the flames. The clearing darkened instantly, and the hot, acrid stench of wet ash overwhelmed every other smell. Sweat prickled her upper lip, and she wiped her mouth with the back of her hand. It did no good. "Where you staying?"

"What the hell do you care?"

Flak shook her head. "Just wondered how you got here so fast."

"I'm the one called it in. I live right there." He pointed over his right shoulder to another frame and tin structure about thirty yards away. The crazed shadows from the drowning fire obscured it from moment to moment.

Flak found herself twisting at the empty ring finger of her left hand. She forced her hands onto her hips and tilted her chin up so she could see his face. "So, what woke you up?"

"Oh, I was awake already. But it was too late to do anything." He stopped to take a drag off his cigarette. Flak motioned to keep him talking.

"The little gal that was with me got up to go to the bathroom. I heard a muffled thud, sort of a 'whoomp' sound. Probably the gas going up. Then she started squalling—by the time I looked out the front window, the house was a torch.

I told her to call 911, headed over this way, and about that time the roof caved in. I went back in and put on some clothes and waited for the fire department to get here."

He stomped the half-smoked cigarette out with a vicious twist of his boot.

"So who's the 'little gal'?" Flak tried to keep the interest in her voice at the professional level.

"You know what, Sheriff? I never even asked her what her name was."

Flak's question came out a little too quick and a little too shrill for her own taste. "She still here?"

"No, ma'am, she's not." He still stared at the fire, but his lip quirked, just for a split second.

Flak forced as much calm reason as she could dig up into her next words. "I'm going to need her name—she's a witness."

"Tough."

"Damn it, Curtis Lee! I need that woman's name!" She felt the heels of her boots come off the ground, like she was trying to make herself taller to intimidate him. She folded her arms, and settled back to the ground.

He took one step away. "Don't you flap let that red-head temper at me, little girl, I'm telling the truth."

"You're lying." Flak forced the words out between gritted teeth.

"No, I ain't. All I know is that when she left here, she was headed home to her husband and kids. Even if I did know her name, I wouldn't tell you."

"Yeah, that's you—never kiss and tell, right? Always a gentleman." The mostly involuntary sarcasm in her voice would have laid a layer of frost across a lesser man.

"Well we wasn't exactly kissing at that particular moment." He lifted an eyebrow. "What was she a witness to, anyway? You saying somebody set this fire deliberate? That's just a load of bulls... horse hockey."

"Why do you say that?"

He gestured at the quenched building. "The old bas—the old man smoked two or three packs of Camels a day. He had scars on his hands from letting them burn too far." Curt shook his head. "I warned him a hundred times about smoking in bed. He never listened to nothing. He set his own self on fire."

"You sure about that?"

He nodded as he spoke. "I ain't sure about much, but I'd place a bet on that one."

She looked down at her boots and back at the fire fighters. The only light in the clearing now was from her cruiser and the fire engines. The circling colors lit up the reflective tape on the protective suits, and bounced in crazy angles across the water they poured on the smoking ruin. Suddenly, the radio clipped to her left shoulder board crackled.

"Sheriff, you copy?"

She reached across her chest, grabbed the combination receiver/microphone with her right hand, and tilted her chin down to answer. "10-4."

"We got a domestic disturbance off of San Augustine Highway—you might want to go take a look-see."

She keyed the mike. "Dang it, Dorrie, would you use the codes?"

"Yes, ma'am. We got a 10-16 on Boozer Street." The dispatcher's voice was dry, businesslike.

Flak sighed, and spoke in the receiver once more. "I'm on my way."

She glared at the half-naked man, who continued to watch the fire fighters. "Until I get a report from the investigator, I have to treat this as a crime scene." She shook her head, more at herself than him, and tried to tamp down the anger in her voice. "If you don't give me that woman's name, you have no alibi. That makes you a suspect."

Flak turned on her heel and stalked away with as much dignity as she could muster up. Knowing he was looking at her rear-end while she was walking didn't help. She couldn't believe he'd let her get the last word.

He didn't. "Well then, I 'suspect' we'll be seeing a lot of each other, won't we, Sheriff!"

With her back still to Curt, she paused in front of Garvey. "Look, I'll be back as soon as I can. Did you call the state?"

"Yep. Soon as I heard there might be someone in the house, I got Dorrie on the line to Houston investigation office. It'll take him about three hours to get here." The big man finally looked down at her. "You going to get some sleep?"

She looked at the no-nonsense Timex on her left wrist. "No—the paper mill folks got their paychecks about eight hours ago now. If I get there quick enough, I might keep Jasper Jay from getting his bell rung too bad."

He looked at his own wristwatch, "You better move; it's already past two. You tell Faith-Ann I said 'Hey.'"

"Don't let your boys drown my evidence any more than they have to, Garv."

He grinned. "Anybody ever tell you to stop teaching your grandma to suck eggs? Fires are my business, girl. Now git."

She smiled back at him. "Sorry, Garv. Long night."

The big man shook his head. "And getting longer by the minute."

As she rounded one of many curves back toward Nacogdoches, Flak paid more attention to her thoughts than to the long-familiar road. Four years of avoiding Curt hadn't diminished his ability to upset her. He could still push her from zero to pissed off in two seconds flat.

The road straightened into the more developed area just outside the Loop. Flak left the lights flashing, punched the button for the siren, and then floored the accelerator to push the cruiser up the entrance ramp heading northwest.

She couldn't get Curt out of her mind, but that had never been easy. With the city's population of only thirty thousand, she couldn't entirely avoid him. She had learned after a while not to let the sight of his beat-up, paint-speckled pickup ruin her day, but she had earned what little peace of mind she had attained the hard way.

After she turned onto the San Augustine Highway, Flak kept an eye peeled for the little blacktop road. She hadn't pulled "JJ duty" since she'd made sheriff and moved to day shift. Jasper Jay Rawlins was married to Faith-Ann Jones, who happened to be a second cousin once removed to the prior sheriff.

Faith-Ann's strict upbringing in what most folks in Nacogdoches called the 'Postolic Church gave the woman little patience with drinking and drunkards. It was too bad she married a man who regularly spent half his paycheck in the local bars every other Friday night.

The combination of her religion's prohibition of divorce, along with its permission to rebuke the sinner, left Jasper Jay in danger of gross bodily harm every payday. As soon as he sobered up, he always refused to press charges, so "JJ duty" became established routine.

Plant paydays found an officer in the parking lot of Jasper Jay's favorite hangout at closing time to get him off the streets before he got a DUI.

The duty had fallen to Flak tonight, subbing for an absent deputy, but the fire delayed her just long enough to let him get home first, dang it. No telling what kind of damage he'd done to mailboxes and garbage cans and anything else on the way. Of course, he didn't drive all that well sober, either.

Lyndon Jones had protected Jasper Jay out of family obligation, but Flak continued trying to figure some way to stop using county resources to save his bacon. She had yet to come up with anything that would suffice. Maybe the next sheriff would solve the problem. If there was a next sheriff. She grinned at the thought of retiring in office, like Lyndon had before her. Hopefully the large belly he'd grown while in office wasn't a requirement.

Faith-Ann's shouts pierced the cruiser's open window before Flak got the vehicle fully in the circular gravel drive. The single-wide trailer's small, whitewashed front porch looked shiny and new in the headlights. Flak remembered climbing up rickety black metal stairs before, the kind where you knocked, and then backed down a step or two to keep the door from smacking you when it opened.

"Faith-Ann?" Flak tapped once, and then opened the front door of the trailer house.

"Faith-Ann, calm down!"

If one quick glance was enough to judge, the cramped living room hadn't changed one little bit since her last visit.

The praying hands bookends still sat on the fake mantelpiece with only one book—the Good Book— between them. The loud flower pattern of the couch gleamed, unfaded, beneath its plastic slipcover. Frilly lampshades still sported their plastic covers as well. A duct-tape-patched recliner, tilting gently to one side, remained the only unprotected piece of furniture in the room. Its occupant leaned the same direction as the chair.

Across the room, the woman raged, undeterred by Flak's entry. "You raggedy, no-good, beer-swilling, skirt-chasing, two-timing, redneck, low-life drunk, why do you even come home?" Flak knew she'd made it in time—Faith-Ann still exercised her vocabulary on her husband rather than the nearest weapon.

"I loooooove you, Faithie," crooned her tirade's cross-eyed target. "I got to come home to my angel baby sweetie pie honey doodle." Jasper Jay's professions of love always seemed miraculous to Flak. Drunk or sober, the little man was always willing to share his undying affection for his wife with anyone who would listen long enough.

"Okay, man, it's time to go." Flak grabbed one of his limp arms, ducked under it, and used it to shoulder Jasper Jay out of his chair. His five-foot, nine-inch, hundred-and-thirty-pound frame felt like a sack of bones.

A few short feet away, arms folded under a formidable bosom, Faith-Ann was twice her husband's width and almost as tall. She filled most of the kitchen doorway, and her piled-up Pentecostal hairdo took up the rest.

The man continued his love talking as Flak half-walked, half-dragged him to the outer door. She nodded to Faith-Ann. "Somebody'll run him back in the morning. Chief Garvey sends his regards."

Faith-Ann's harangue continued, unabated, now with one hand raised as if witnessing in church. "One day, Jasper Jay Rawlins. One fine day, there won't be any earthly law that'll save your sinful backside. The Lord himself will visit his wrath upon you!" On that cheerful note, Flak exited, and gently shut the door with a backwards shove of one foot. It muted the sermon a little.

She struggled to pour the bony little man into the back seat of the cruiser, but he kept slithering back out, moaning for his Faithie. "This is like trying to get stinky pudding back in the bowl," she muttered, as he oozed out the door for the third time.

"I loooooove puddin'."

"Yeah, bud, you looooove everything when you're drunk." She pushed him completely over into the seat, folded his legs up and out of the way and eased the door shut. She rounded the vehicle.

Sliding behind the steering wheel, she picked up the mike and keyed it as she slammed her door shut with the other hand. "Sheriff to dispatch. I got a 10-95. Have Jerry meet me outside." The "10-4" sounded tinny and far away. Reception always got iffy in the rural areas. As she pulled back on the highway, she wondered if Jasper Jay ever clicked to the irony of residing on Boozer Street.

"Aw, you don't need Jerry. I ain't drunk, Flak, I'm just feeling goooood."

In her rearview mirror, she saw him lean his head against the mesh. "Flak, Flak, Flak. Why'd your mama name you Flak, anyway?" The question rode on a breath reeking of whiskey and vomit. She waved her hand in front of her nose.

"Whew! Back up off that screen, Jasper Jay. Mama didn't name me Flak, and you been asking me that question ever since I made deputy. I've answered it a hundred times."

"No, I ain't done no such a thing. Naw. Not me, Flak. Feels funny in my mouth. Flak. Flak. Flak."

From long experience, she knew he wouldn't stop. "My initials are AAA—and the boys in third grade made noises like a machine gun at me all the time. I went crying to Daddy, and he just said they were giving me a bunch of flak. He thought it was funny." She shrugged, unwilling to tell him the hard part—that she used the nickname to honor the father she lost only a few years later. "I been called that ever since."

"AAA, huh? But, but Flak don't start with no A."

"Damn it, Jasper Jay, shut up. I know better than to talk to you."

"Ooooohhh, you're cussing! Faithie don't like it when people cuss. I love my Faithie darlin'; she's my sugar pie baby lumpkin." Her glance in the rearview showed his face sliding down the screen as his words slowed like an old record player. He finally slumped out of sight. She hoped he wouldn't wake up again before she got to the county jail.

When she pulled into the lot, the biggest jailer in East Texas stood in front of the parking spot marked "Reserved for Sheriff." She got out of the cruiser; put her hat on, swivel-hipped the door shut in one graceful motion and left the drunk to Jerry's tender ministrations with a brief "Thanks" to the big man.

One small mercy in pulling the night shift—the angle of the lights above left the box-shaped facility in darkness. The architect who built it must have had a grudge against the county; it looked like it had been built with children's building blocks and spit. The old county courthouse may not have been beautiful, but it had character.

Flak held the metal and glass door open as the huge jailer pulled Jasper Jay out of the car by the waistband of his jeans and then slung him over his shoulder like a sack of feed. Jerry nodded to Flak as he strode past her with his skinny, smelly burden and down the hall to the jail section.

CHAPTER TWO

Jenny

I have no memories of my father until I was around six years old. No, really, it's true. He just isn't in my head until then. Don't know why.

It isn't like I didn't know he existed. I knew he was out there, a presence somewhere, but I just have no pictures in my head of him before I started school. I remember Mama boiling his work clothes on the stove, in a big, black-speckled steel pot. She claimed it was the only way she could get most of the paint out of them. For a four-year-old, of course, it was fall-down funny to see her pulling clothes off the stove instead of food.

The time with Mama when I was between four and six years old, after my sister started school—those were probably the best years of life. There were five of us, and until then, I'd never had my mother's undivided attention. I loved every minute of it.

Now, don't get me wrong, Mama was no saint. In fact, the reason I didn't go to kindergarten was 'because somebody pissed her off. Some of it I remember, and some of it is family stories, but I can't tell you where I leave off and they begin.

Anyway, this lady named Miz Whitaker comes to the door selling Amway or Avon or some such thing. It took my mother like an hour to get rid of her just 'cause she didn't want to be rude. Well, about an hour later, another lady comes to the door and says her name is Miz Whitaker, and she wants to enroll me in kindergarten. Preschool they'd call it now, I guess.

Mama figured the first one had ratted her out to the second one for having a kid at home. So she tells this second lady that she saw no reason to enroll her daughter in a useless year of school, just so she could be taught to play nice with the little black children. Only she didn't say it near that nice.

Come to find out the two ladies were no relation—every third person around there carried the last name of Whitaker.

Don't want you to think Mama was bigoted. This happened back in '67, and they'd just integrated the Texas schools. Actually, she probably was bigoted. She was raised that way. Believe me, you didn't grow up white in Texas in that time, and not grow up prejudiced. She grew out of it in her later years.

What really pissed her off about the whole thing with the Whitaker women, though, was that they kept interrupting her "stories." You know, the soap operas. Mama loved 'em. She and I used to sit and watch them together. Well, I would. I'd curl up on the couch, and she'd pull out the ironing board and get that done while General Hospital or All my Children was on.

Sometimes I'd put my feet on this old bass drum that Mama had varnished and we used as a coffee table. Before the varnish was dry, our cat walked across the top of it, leaving perfect little cat prints behind. I can see it almost as clear as her ironing. I can smell the hot metal scent of the starch and the damp clean of the shirts. She had a Coca-Cola bottle with a sprinkler top, and she'd sprinkle all the clothes, and then wrap them up in a towel. This was either before steam irons or before we could afford one. Damping down the clothes got the iron steaming enough to smooth out the wrinkles without burning. We'd watch the stories, and Mama would talk to the characters like they were real—like they were her friends, warning them that something bad was going to happen. Sometimes she'd turn on Dark Shadows, a mildly scary soap opera. I just loved Barnabas Collins—I thought he was the scariest man in the world.

And that was that. That's how our days went together. By the time the soaps were done, my brothers and sisters would get off the school bus, and by then, dinner needed starting. Those were the last few years before Daddy started taking her to work with him. It was like the calm before the storm.

CHAPTER THREE

Flak knew the sun was up, but the curtain of tall pines bordering the back of the clearing kept the now-smoldering ruin in semi-darkness. The trees seemed to lean forward, watching the human activity with an ancient curiosity.

She pulled her cruiser bumper to bumper with the fire chief's car. Sitting on his hood, arms folded, Garvey patted the red metal next to him in mute invitation. The uncertain light shadowed another, unfamiliar car off to one side. She leaned against the bumper of the chief's car and got her first good look at the destruction that had been hidden in the full dark a few hours earlier. He motioned with his chin toward the flashlight beam moving around the wreckage. "Investigator's been off in there since the last truck left."

"You been out here all night long?"

"Yeah, pretty much. Did you get Jasper Jay out alive?"

"Uh-huh." She shook her head. "That woman will kill him one day."

"Oh, I don't imagine so. Faith-Ann's all talk and no walk. She just wants to put the fear of God into him, not send him to meet his Maker." Garvey always seemed to see the best in people, even ones that didn't deserve the consideration, in her opinion.

She shook her head. "I don't know, man."

The screen door on Curtis Lee's house slammed, and a pale shape headed toward the car. Curt stopped in front of her, dressed head to toe in painter's whites. She caught a faint, familiar whiff of Old Spice aftershave, even through the smell of smoke and charred wood. That same ache took shape in her chest. What would it take to make it finally stop?

"When are y'all going to get him out of there?" He jerked his head toward the ruin.

"Hang on to a little bit of hope, son." Garvey's deep drawl offered solace. "Maybe you're wrong— maybe he took off somewhere and didn't tell you. My mama used to say, 'Don't trouble trouble 'til trouble troubles you.'"

"No disrespect to your mama, Garv, but you're a little late on that one." Curt lit a cigarette, turned his head away and blew a cloud of smoke away from them. "Look, I got to go finish this lady's house up this morning. Soon as I get done there, I'll be back."

"Still hope you're wrong about him being in there, Curtis Lee. But if he is, well, I'm real sorry." Garvey shook his head slow. "It's a bad way to lose your daddy."

"If you're really sorry, bubba, you'll probably be the only one in the county." Curt turned without further goodbye and strode across the wet grass toward his old truck.

Flak scooted further up on the hood of Garvey's car and hooked her boot heels onto the bumper to keep from sliding off. Unlike Garvey, she couldn't keep both feet on the ground and stay comfortably seated.

"Did you know Tucker?" she asked Garvey idly, watching the light beam move around the blackened debris, accompanied by frequent bright explosions from a camera.

"Sure, didn't you?" He sounded surprised. "You are his daughter-in-law."

She shook her head. "No, not really. Curt wouldn't go around him when we were together. Never said why."

Actually, there were a lot of things her husband had never said. Among them, the words "I love you." Neither of them had ever said it.

She was too proud to say it before he did, and too stubborn to ask him whether he loved her or not. Even in their civil ceremony, love was never mentioned. She shook her head to try to get back to the present.

The chief was saying, "Aw, Tucker was just a good old boy, as far as I ever knew." Garvey put one hand to his back for a moment, and stretched, wincing.

"He taught Curtis Lee to paint, I know that much, but anything else I knew about him I heard from Maggie. You might want to ask her."

"Maggie? The oldest daughter, right? I only met her once or twice." Curt hadn't just kept her away from Tucker; he'd kept her away from the whole family pretty much. Asking him if he was ashamed of her had started a big old fight, but he never had answered the question, as she recalled. Looking back, she wondered if the fight was just to distract her.

The chief continued. "Yeah, the oldest girl. I dated her a couple of times. She married some military fella back in the early '80s, followed him over the world, and then came back to Texas some years back when he was done with his hitch. She used to visit more when Miz Emlyn was still alive."

"You knew Miz Emlyn?" Flak decided she shouldn't be surprised. Nacogdoches County's population was small, by any standards, and it seemed like you couldn't throw a rock without hitting somebody's relative.

"Everybody that was raised around Cushing knew her. She was a neat little lady. I went to school in Douglass, down the road, but Miz Emlyn threw me out of the church nursery when I was six." He grinned. "She didn't put up with much."

Flak wondered if Garvey knew anything about Emlyn and Tucker's marriage. She had her suspicions, from a few things Curt had said, but had never confirmed any of them. When she'd asked Curt why he seldom went to see Tucker, and never took her with him when he did visit, he only said "I wouldn't take a female dog near the old man, much less my wife."

So she asked Garvey, "Do you know why she and Tucker divorced?"

He shook his head. "No, not really. It might have come up, but I was still pretty young. I think it was back in the '70s sometime, late '70s maybe."

She asked, "Do you know where Maggie's living now?"

Nodding, "Somebody told me she up and bought that little burned-out store in Looneyville."

"I was just-"

"Hey, Chief," yelled the investigator.

"Yeah?"

"Go ahead and call the removal folks—I'll walk 'em through how to get each piece out of here."

"You got it, Jim," Garvey pulled his lanky form off the hood with a grunt.

The morning light that brightened from moment to moment showed her the investigator, who straightened and put a sooty hand to his cover-alled back.

Pushing his glasses up must be a habit, she decided, as he walked toward her. His nose was black-smudged, but the rest of his face was clean.

"What's the verdict?"

"Ah, Sheriff, is it?" Flak introduced herself, and he started to shake her hand, but looked at his grubby paw and visibly decided against it.

"Well, I couldn't get to the body, if there is one, because of the roof collapse. But the greatest concentration of debris is right over the sleeping area." The scant-haired, thin gentleman pointed toward the center of the fire damage, where sheets of blackened corrugated tin lay in a crazed, heaped mass.

"I can tell you there are signs of some kind of occurrence before the fire."

"What signs?"

"Well, the glass blew out of almost every window, consistent with some kind of explosion, probably shortly after the fire began, because there's little smoke marking them. In the bathroom window, though, the glass was fully exposed to the smoke and heat, and inside the perimeter of the house."

Flak squinted, "So something came through the window? Like a firebomb?"

"Or somebody. Maybe it was just broke before the fire and not fixed. I won't know much 'til we get that roof material out of there, and I may not know then."

"How about accelerants?"

He shook his head. "Can't give you anything on that right now. I'll take the glass back to my lab, should have the results for you in a week, maybe two." He smiled at her, "If the good Lord's willing and the creeks don't rise, you know."

She watched the removal team help Jim piece through and shift the wreckage until she couldn't stay awake, then stretched out in her cruiser's back seat, one ear open for the radio traffic. Leaving the door open, she drifted off, hat tilted over her face for shade.

When someone lifted the hat, she came awake in a big hurry. Curt leaned in the window she'd left open by her head, his face upside down in her bleary vision. She sat up, grabbed her hat, and then scrambled out of the vehicle, rubbing her eyes.

"Dang it, Curt, couldn't you just—" She stopped at the sight of the rearranged ruins. Piles of corrugated tin made neat rows beyond the site of the fire, and four men stood in one spot near the center of the devastation.

Curt came around the vehicle. "Garvey said to wake you up. Come on." He walked past her.

"Wait, Curt. Look." She grabbed the back of his t-shirt and used it to swing past him. "You don't want to see this. Especially if your dad's there."

"Shut up, Sheriff." But he let her take the lead.

The four men in the middle of the foul-smelling rubble stood shoulder to shoulder. Their positions created an impromptu wall, which Flak edged around, Curt close on her heels.

The stark outline of a charred human shape rested in the tangled chaos of the bed, both hands near the head. She prayed the old man had slept that way, that he'd never known what hit him.

"Oh, God," Curt said. Flak's quick glance showed her his tanned face had turned gray. The pair from the removal team recited the Lord's Prayer in a low whisper.

"I've got to get the coroner out here, Curt. Why don't you walk me to the car?"

"Yeah."

"Who might have wanted to kill Tucker?" Flak asked some hours later. The coroner left near noon, along with the chief, and the removal team took the corpse with them, mercifully concealed in a black body bag.

The fire inspector headed back to Houston with a trunk full of labeled samples shortly after.

Flak and Curt sat on the tailgate of his pickup, faced away from the sight of the ruined house. An occasional breeze cooled her sweaty face, but brought the acid smell of burned wood with it, and dark undertones of scorched meat.

She resolutely ignored the smells, and hoped they masked her own forty-eight-hours-past-a-shower aroma. She turned around on the metal surface so she could see him, knowing she was grinding even more dirt into her already-ruined uniform pants.

Curt rubbed at his eyes with the heel of his hands, obviously exhausted, and took a drag from his ever-present cigarette. "Anybody. Everybody who ever really knew him probably wanted to kill him."

"Come on, Curt—everybody?"

He nodded, and exhaled a lungful of smoke into the rancid air. "Far as I ever knew."

She wondered how far she could push him before he started pushing back. "Does that include you?"

Curt didn't answer immediately, but Flak knew if she remained silent, he'd start talking soon. Pushing down the memories of the many fights they had, she kept her eyes on his face.

The profile was still the same—a little more weather-beaten, perhaps, but the bump on the bridge of his nose from the punch he'd taken in a bar fight was still there. His usually clear brown eyes were muddy-looking now, flooded with some emotion she couldn't identify.

"Every one of his kids wanted to kill him at some point in their lives, and most of his wives." His words came out slow, as if remembering. "But I don't think any of us had actually considered it for a long time. I know I haven't thought about it much recently."

"What do you mean?"

He shook his head, as if she'd asked a stupid question. "Exactly what I said."

"Look, Curt, my job is to find out who killed your daddy. Would you help me out some?" She struggled to keep the anger out of her voice, tried to remember he'd just lost his father, but knew she was losing the battle.

He said, "You don't know yet he *was* killed, do you?"

"There's evidence someone else may have been in the house."

"What evidence?" Curt asked. He dropped his cigarette over the edge of the tailgate, and stomped it into the damp red clay with a boot heel before he sat back down.

"I'm not going to discuss it with you."

Off the pickup he came again, and wheeled to face her. "Stop treating me like a criminal! I didn't kill my daddy. I was too busy saving his ass to kill him."

She stayed silent.

"That house, or what's left of it, belongs to me."

Flak avoided the arm he swung and pointed at the gutted building, but couldn't avoid the anger in his eyes.

His voice, laced with anger, rose to a shout.

"Everything he owned belonged to me. Three years ago, I got him out of a leaky old tent down near Sam Rayburn Lake, put him in that house, found him a car, took him to the doctor and made sure he got his Social Security every month. I did everything in the world for him, damn you! And I did not kill him."

"Then who did?" Flak refused to let him intimidate her. They'd had some serious fights before she moved out on him, but no matter how angry he got, Curt would never hit a woman. Or at least, she was pretty sure he wouldn't.

"Nobody killed him, damn it! He killed himself smoking in bed."

Flak shifted tactics. "Seen any of your family lately?"

"Why? You think one of them did it? I thought you decided I'd killed him." The acid in his voice brought back that persistent ache in her chest. She didn't want him to hate her, but her job demanded the questions.

"I just heard that Maggie had moved back to the area, that's all." She kept her tones even, trying to moderate his anger, if only a little. If someone really had killed the old man, she needed to keep him talking to ever have a chance to figure it out.

"Yeah?"

"Did she come to visit you or Tucker?

A slow flush darkened his face even further.

"I know I didn't take you around the rest of the family much when we were together. So you might not think I'm close to my brothers and sisters. But if you think for one single, solitary second I'm going to sit here and pin what you're calling murder on my family, you're nuts."

His arms folded, he looked like the end of every fight they'd ever had, walled-off, untouchable.

She went back on the attack, since moderation hadn't worked. Pushing all the sarcasm she could into her voice, "Why was it your job to rescue Tucker, anyway? Where were the rest of the kids when he needed them?"

Curt retrieved another cigarette instead of answering. He held the filter between his little finger and ring finger on his right hand, and manipulated the lighter with his left.

The fingers of the right hand stayed stiff, covering most of his face every time he took a drag.

"What happened to your hand, Curt?"

"I cut it off."

"Would you answer one question straight?"

He took a deep breath. "I put it through a glass shower door."

"Accidentally?" All she wanted to do was stop hammering at him, but it was her job to keep pushing until something, or somebody, broke. It surprised her a bit to realize she hoped he wouldn't.

His voice brought back memories of that comic who made the phrase "Here's your sign!" popular.

"No, it was on purpose—I was just itching to find out what all them tendons and muscles looked like on the inside."

"When did you do it?"

"Four years ago this week."

"Why were you shoving your fist through a shower door?"

"None of your stinking business. Had nothing to do with you, nothing to do with this. In fact, I believe I've answered plenty of your questions for one day."

He used both hands to push himself off the tailgate to a standing position in one smooth motion.

After a few steps toward his house, he pulled the cigarette out of his mouth, and turned to face her.

"I know you got a job to do, Neets," he said, using the nickname he'd given her during their early days together. "But that old man ain't worth the county's time or money."

He turned again, and this time, kept walking.

"He was worth yours," she whispered.

CHAPTER FOUR
Jenny

On the bad days, I'd go under the old frame house with my sister and draw in the dry, fine dirt or play with the stuffed animals and toys we left under there.

The house was built on pilings on the side of a hill. The front sat right on the ground, but the back of the house was, well it was high enough that I could walk under it at the age of six without bending.

All the walls were one-by-twelve boards, with no insulation or wallpaper or anything, just the paint that Mama slapped on every chance she got. The floors were one-by-fours, suspended across the pilings, with knotholes every once in a while. We sat and listened to the deep voice getting louder and louder above, and we stayed real quiet. You could hear every word, though it was muffled some. Don't remember what the fight was about that particular time. Didn't matter, anyway.

I didn't know I was shaking until my sister put a hand on my arm. It was amazing there, in our little under house world, how the sense of threat permeated that huge structure above us. It was soaked in it, like a waterlogged raft in an ocean of fear. Eventually, a slap rang out. My sister and I both flinched at the sound—it was like the report of a gun. But at least the shouting stopped.

We crawled out from our safe place and went in to dinner. Not the first time we were called, but the second time. Sometimes we waited until the third or fourth yell of "Girls, dinner time!" before we headed inside.

My sis jumped onto the unrailed front porch, and I followed close behind her. I was always close behind her. We went in the house through the living room screen door, letting it slam behind us, and then we took the long way around to the kitchen.

With no hallways, the only choices were to go through the bathroom or through Mama and Daddy's bedroom. The bedroom always smelled of him, a mix of paint thinner, sweat and aftershave overwhelming the fainter smell of Mama's perfume. We always went the other way.

He was there at the table, still in his painter's whites, always so much bigger than anyone else in the room. His huge hands lay quiet on the table on both sides of his empty plate. He looked up, "You come the first time your mama calls you, you hear me?"

We nodded at the same time and said, "Yes, sir," but he wasn't angry any more, you could tell. He had this satisfied look, like he did when he finished a job.

Mama's face was colored up, all red, but she didn't say anything. That was nothing unusual to us. When Mama did speak, it was sparingly, with no hand movements and little emotion. She moved back and forth without wasted effort along the stove and the kitchen cabinets.

Her hair was almost completely gray, and rolled up in her usual French knot. Also, as usual, some of it escaped along the sides of her face, a few wisps loosened by the heat or by something worse.

My sis sat down on one side of our father and I sat on the other. All three boys sat on the opposite side of the table.

Mama turned from the stove toward the table with a pot in her hand, and I could see the imprint of fingers on her cheek. I looked down at my plate really quick. I was pretty sure that was something I wasn't supposed to notice.

I glimpsed a movement to my right and it made me jump just a little. When I turned my head, his hand was moving toward my face. I could see the faint white of old paint in the lines and creases of his palm.

With an effort that made my toes clench under the table, I held still. He ran his finger down my jaw from earlobe to chin. The smell of work and sweat cut through the warm, familiar kitchen scents.

"You look an awful lot like your mother."

The bang of a serving spoon on a plate made him and me both jump, and he turned back toward his plate. I looked at Mama. I could tell she was mad, but I didn't know why. She never said a word, just finished dishing up dinner.

CHAPTER FIVE

Flak snatched the fax out of the machine the second it finished printing. She read it three times, and finally called the Houston fire investigation offices.

"Jim, I don't understand this report at all."

"Well, it's almost all zeros, anyway. There was an accelerant present—we found it in trace amounts in a few of the samples in the bathroom. I don't know if it degraded fast, or was simply weak to begin with. Our gas chromatograph is drawing a blank." His voice sounded discouraged.

Flak wasn't much on looking stupid, but this was way beyond her range of knowledge. "Can you tell me what that means?"

"The short answer? Every major fuel facility in the United States submits graphs and material safety data sheets to the database we use to identify accelerants. This is either of foreign make, or it's something that's in research and development now. I can tell you what some of the active elements are. I know it's an accelerant simply because it's got some of the right ingredients, but there's not a sheet out there on it. We just don't know what it is or where it came from yet. Sorry."

"Well, you know I have to ask the question. Did somebody actually set that fire?"

"Most likely. But unless you've come up with some kind of physical evidence like fingerprints, I couldn't testify at this point that it wasn't the victim." His discouraged voice made her wince.

She tried to come up with something encouraging, but gave up. "Well, crap."

"I know, Sheriff. We're still working it."

"Okay—thanks, Jim."

"Wish I could have been more help."

"So do I."

An hour so later, Flak turned the Crown Vic's front wheels to the right at the stop sign where Farm-to-Market Road 343 met FM 225, and then steered left a hundred yards later into the pea gravel parking lot at the old Looneyville store.

From the road, the new two-by-fours at the once-white building's back corner stood out in sharp contrast to the smoke-damaged walls and peeling paint of the rest of the structure. She knew there had been a small fire that discouraged the last owners—that must have been where it did the worst damage. She had heard the couple handed the keys over to the bank and headed back to San Antonio or Austin or wherever it was they'd come from.

A fifty-foot long, single-wide trailer sat to the left of the store, toward the back. The front doors of each building faced toward the road. The mobile home wasn't damaged like store, but was marked up by smoke on the end nearest the new construction. The parking lot stretched in front of both.

Flak walked under the dilapidated canopy, listening to the sound of her boot heels change from the crunch of the gravel to the tik-tok of the smoother concrete where cars had once parked to fill up with gas. The old pumps had been removed long since, evidenced by the rusted pipe stubs emerging from the concrete pad to her right.

One of the battered screen doors canted over, held only at the bottom. She opened its partner, flinching at the rusty squeal of the hinges. After trying the knob on the inner door without success, she banged with the heel of her hand on the hollow wood.

"We're not open yet!" a woman's voice yelled. It was hard to tell which direction it came from.

"County Sheriff," Flak yelled in return. "Just want to talk to you a minute."

"Hang on a second." She heard a different female voice ask "What'd she say?", and then the sound of boxes being shoved around. The door clicked and swung open to more shrieks of tortured metal.

The small woman who stood in the opening was smudged with dust from her new-looking jeans to the collar of her once-white shirt. Her dark hair showed signs of getting close to a cobweb or two, and curled near her face from the sweat that accompanied the obvious signs of hard work.

"Well hello, Anita. Come on in—it's a big mess, but we have coffee if you want a cup."

"Hello, Maggie. Long time no see. Yeah, I'd love a cup. Black, please."

"Just stay by the door, it's a rat maze in here. I'll get us both a cup. How's life treating you, anyway?"

Maggie left Flak near the door and wound her way through the dim recesses of the building to a shiny new coffee machine on the back wall.

"Oh, fair to middlin'."

Maggie laughed, "The great Texas catch-all phrase."

"Yeah, I guess. I just use it because I get tired of saying 'fine,' all the time—that, and 'fine' isn't always the truth, either."

Maggie threaded her way back through the boxes scattered around the floor, a steaming cup in each hand, and handed one to Flak. "I wanted to take a break anyway. Why don't we sit outside—there's no place to take the weight off your feet in here yet."

"Sounds good." The sheriff followed the smaller woman out the door, and restrained her flinch at the noise of the screaming hinges.

"Did I hear someone else's voice? I didn't see anybody." Flak tried to find a comfortable spot on the old bench, without notable success. The smell of ancient oil from the attached garage mixed with the scent of new lumber and disturbed dust. She sneezed.

"Gesundheit," Maggie said, after her sip of coffee. "That was Jenny. She'll come out in a minute. She has something in the oven over in the trailer."

Flak hazarded the question. "Your little sister Jenny?"

"Yeah, we're putting all this back together, trying to get it fixed up and back in business."

"What inspired all this?" Flak waved her hand to indicate the store, trailer, and property behind it.

"Oh, it just seemed like good timing. I had finished up a consulting job when I called Frederick up for his birthday, and told him I was looking around for the next thing. He called me back in May and said this place was up for sale again."

"Frederick–the oldest brother?"

The relationships were beginning to emerge from her hazy memory of the holidays she'd spent with the family. It was the only time Curt had taken her around the group, and there had always been such a crowd, it was hard to keep them sorted out.

"No." Maggie smiled. "He's the oldest but one. Ben's the oldest, then Frederick, Curtis Lee, me and Jenny. We're all around two years apart."

Flak took a swig of her coffee and contemplated ways to bring up Tucker's death.

Maggie spoke first. "Why all the interest in the family, Anita? You and Curtis Lee getting back together?"

"Oh, hell no!"

Maggie giggled, probably at the look of horror on Flak's face.

"I'm here about your daddy's death."

Maggie's smile vanished like smoke in a high wind, and along with it, the sense of good will. When the smaller woman's jaw clenched, Flak realized Maggie actually did look like a younger version of her mother. More in the expressions than the shape of her face, but the resemblance was there.

"I should have known this wasn't a courtesy visit. What do you want to know?" The chilliness of Maggie's voice was a stark contrast to the giggle the moment before. Flak gave herself a mental kick for clumsiness.

She tried to soothe the tensions. "I'm just trying to figure out who might have killed him."

"Curtis Lee said he'd killed himself. Accidentally."

"Maybe. Maybe not. So, who might have wanted to kill him?" Flak made a great effort to keep her tone mild, before taking a sip of her coffee.

"I don't know." Maggie's voice had gone cold and quiet.

"That's funny. Curt said every one of Tucker's children and wives hated him. Did that include you?"

Maggie fired right back, "Did Curtis Lee tell you Tucker tried to kill *him* some year's back?"

"Can't say as he mentioned it, no. Were you there?"

Her voice still tight, Maggie said, "No. He said the old man came right over a curb in that old Ford pickup with the camper on it. Tried to run Curtis Lee down, missed him by a hair."

"You trying to tell me Curt had a grudge worth killing for?" Flak couldn't keep the skepticism out of her voice.

Maggie sagged, and the anger in her face faded into defeat. "No more than the rest of us did."

"What, did he try to kill all of you?"

"I think he attacked all of us at one time or another." Maggie's chin was down now, coffee cup abandoned beside her on the bench, both hands holding her up, shoulders nearly to her ears.

"Define attacked." Flak spoke softly.

Shrugging, "You're the expert—you define it."

Flak, stood, and placed her coffee cup on the bench as well. She stepped away from Maggie, toward the remains of the old gas pumps.

Hooking her fingers in her belt loops, elbows akimbo, she turned back. "Look, Maggie, I'm not trying to accuse you of murder."

"Sounds like you are." Maggie was staring down at her feet, didn't meet Flak's eyes.

"I'm just trying to narrow the suspects down from the entire stinking world, okay?"

"What and you want to narrow it to my family? And you expect me to help you with that?" That pointed chin that looked just like Miz Emlyn's was starting to rise. Maggie was getting her dander up, it looked like.

"I just want to know who Tucker was so I can figure out why he died."

Flak knew her frustration was evident in her voice, but good Lord; these people were so closed up. Every time she got in front of one of them, the barriers slammed up.

"It isn't 'who he was' Sheriff, it's 'what he was.'"

Flak felt a sudden urge to twiddle her lips and make bubbling noises. Trying to get a straight answer out of any of Tucker's kids was completely impossible. She sighed. "Okay, then what was he?"

"Evil."

Flak looked at the canopy above her, and rolled that around in her mind. "That's kind of an odd word to use for your own flesh and blood. Everybody has some redeeming qualities."

"Not everybody. You didn't know him."

A door slammed nearby with a metal and rubber thunk. Within moments, Jenny came around the side of the store.

The last time Flak had seen her, she was in church mode, dowdy flowered dress, still overweight from her last pregnancy, with an infant in her arms. The face hadn't aged a bit, but the short skirt and skin-tight tank top showed everything else had changed.

Jenny stopped in front of Flak and moved a bleach-blond lock of her pixie-cut hair to the side in what was apparently a much-practiced gesture.

"Hey, Anita—how's the deputy dawg biz these days?"

Flak couldn't believe the difference in the woman before her and the picture in her memory. "I'm the sheriff now. Can't complain. You're looking good, girl—you lost weight since I saw you last."

"Yeah, it's been like five years, right?"

"Four—I saw y'all last at Miz Emlyn's funeral."

The flirty demeanor left Jenny's stance like Flak had slapped her. She seemed to crumple in on herself.

"Anita's here to talk about Tucker's death," Maggie patted the seat beside her. Jenny sat, and the older sister put an arm around her shoulders, squeezed her to her side.

"What about it?" The younger woman looked up at Flak from under the lock of hair once more in her eyes. Now it seemed more a shield than an irritant.

Flak hadn't meant to bring up Miz Emlyn, and made sure the next words were as gentle as she could make them. "I'm just trying to find out who killed him."

"Who the hell cares? At least he's dead." The blonde straightened at her sister's side, the sparkle coming back into her eyes.

"Hush, honey." Maggie's mother-tiger glare at Flak spoke volumes.

"No, I mean it. Who cares?" Jenny shrugged off her sister's arm, stood face-to-face with Flak, but out of arm's reach. Her hands on her hips mirrored the sheriff's posture.

"If nobody else will say it, I sure will. I'm glad he's dead—the whole world's a better place without him in it.

That's why me and Maggie went to the 'memorial service,'" putting imaginary quotes in the air. "We just wanted to make sure he was dead."

Flak hadn't gone—she didn't figure Curtis Lee wanted her there. But, if Jenny was going to bow up, she figured she'd see what else she could find out. "So, who do you think might have killed him?"

"Oooh, now, that's a good question." Jenny clasped her hands, like a small child intent on a puzzle. "I always figured if any of us could get up the nerve to kill him, it would be Ben."

"Nerve?" Flak made sure to keep Maggie in her peripheral vision. The older woman's knuckles had whitened on the edge of the bench seat. She leaned toward Jenny, but made no move or sound to stop her.

Nodding, "Oh, yes. It would take nerve. The old man told us all the time, if we were going to kill him, we'd better get him on the first shot. He said we wouldn't last long enough to get a second chance."

Jenny's bright and shiny tones were completely at odds with the words. "Let's see—who else? Well, you wanted to poison him, didn't you, Mags? Not me. Poison's too slow, too easy."

Her eyes were focused somewhere past Flak's left ear, her hands still together in front of her but now it seemed as if in prayer.

"Me, I just wanted to tie him down and shoot him slow. First one foot, then a tourniquet around his calf so he wouldn't bleed to death too soon. Then the other foot, then his knees, then his hands. I wanted to hear him scream." Her serene smile at the prospect stunned Flak.

"Jenny. Jenny! Don't you have something cooking?" Maggie interrupted the younger woman's trance.

"Oh my stars! My cake!" Jenny fled for the trailer.

Flak entered into a staring contest with Maggie, and watched her come to some decision.

"Sheriff, I know what you think you just heard, but you're wrong. She didn't—she couldn't have killed him."

"You sure about that?"

Maggie's voice begged for Flak's understanding. "The medication she's on keeps her attention span at about that of a two-year-old. No way she could keep it together long enough to set somebody on fire. Besides, she was with me the night Tucker died." She continued looking Flak straight in the eye.

It was hard to doubt her sincerity, but Flak had to say it anyway. "I never said he was set on fire."

The older woman shook her head. "Oh, come on! This is East Texas. I found out before it even made the Daily Sentinel."

Flak asked her straight out, "Will she say she was with you the night of the fire?"

A tentative shake of her head from the other woman, "I'm not sure she really remembers dates that clearly."

"Why's she medicated, anyway?" Flak knew she was prying into something Maggie didn't want to divulge, but she was sick of tiptoeing around these people and getting nothing but a runaround.

A stronger head shake from Maggie, "It's not important."

"It might be," Flak put her hands in her pockets, prepared to stay as long as it took.

Again the staring contest, and again, Flak won. Maggie spoke first. "We all have our wounds, Sheriff. Some of us scarred over better than others, but we're all damaged in some way."

Flak pushed her as hard as she felt she could at this stage. "Maggie, I need to know what Jenny's taking and why."

"Then ask her." Yet one more shrug. Flak was getting a little tired of shrugs.

"I'll do that."

When she drove away after a few conventional departure clichés, Flak's rearview mirror showed Maggie, still seated on the bench, drop her head into her hands. It was hard to tell, but it looked like her shoulders were shaking, either from laughter or tears.

Flak lost sight of her when she took the sharp left to head back to town. An empty signpost reminded her she needed to order new signs for the Looneyville town limits,

The college kids at Stephen F. Austin kept stealing them.

CHAPTER SIX

Jenny

Honestly, you couldn't win. If you told him you hadn't done anything, then you got hit for lying. If you told him you had done something, then you got beaten for whatever transgression you'd committed that particular day.

One thing it left me with was a deep understanding of why people run from the cops even when they're not guilty of anything. Everybody's guilty of something.

So, anyway, we're all lined up, hands behind our backs, and he always starts with the oldest. I'm down at the end of the line, so there's plenty of time to wait while the boys get what he thinks they deserve for either doing something or lying about doing nothing.

Out of the corner of my eye, I see my sis standing ramrod straight beside me. The look on her face is absolutely poker flat. Not me. I was shaking and crying before he ever got to the second brother. By the time he got to me, I'd be a weepy, snotty mess. It was absolutely deliberate on my part, while still being how I actually felt. It's hard to explain that if you haven't been there.

I realize the shaking's getting worse this time, but there's nothing I can do about it. I see sis cut her eyes over at me under her lashes, but she can't do anything about it either. She can't even turn her head. If she does, we'll be both be smacked for conspiring against him. The stripes on my butt

45

hadn't disappeared from the last whipping.

By the time he got to me, his belt-swinging hand was tired, so he let me off with a warning. The crying didn't work every time, but it was always worth a try to save my skin.

I know my sister envied me my ability to cry at the drop of a hat, because she told me she did. Bless her heart, that well went dry for her really early. That was the reason why she was the one who ended up with a shotgun pointed at her head later on, and I ended up stuck with him.

She felt really guilty for leaving me there, but she would have been stupid not to take the chance to escape. I never felt like she did the wrong thing by going when she did.

Anyway, back to the line ups. The worst ever was the metal detector. He had purchased this thing, which was very high tech at the time and I'm sure extremely expensive, to hunt for belt buckles and such at his family's graveyard near his old home place down close to Lufkin. He pulls it out of the box one Saturday morning a few months after he got it, and the round bottom plate is hanging on by its wires.

That was bad. That line up lasted for hours. As weepy and snotty as I was, I still got whipped that day. Every one of us got beaten during that particular tirade, but nobody admitted to damaging the stupid thing. Most unusual. Somebody almost always copped to the transgression of the day.

Years later, Mama told me she figured he'd been angry when he put it in the box, and slammed it in there instead of placing it in there carefully. Just as well she didn't say that at the time—he'd have said she broke it and was covering for herself with a lie, and God knows what he would have done to her. He accused her of covering up for us all the time. She didn't when I was very young, but as we got older, she did.

Mama told me she thought for decades he was out of control when he'd go into one of his rages. But near the end of things, he was mad at my sister for running away, which she did about every six months or so after she turned fourteen. He went raging through the house breaking stuff.

Well, Mama always bought the two of us stuff that looked alike. He picked up a tape recorder, one of those little flat cassette recorder things and asked Mama if it was my sister's. She had no idea, but she said no, it was mine. He set it down very carefully, and went on to the next thing to break it.

That's when she said she finally decided it was all a game on his part. Less blame could be attached to a man out of control, so he chose to make us believe. We believed a lot of things that were dead wrong.

What it amounted to, though, with the line ups and pretty much every other interaction with dear old Dad, was, if you weren't saying what he wanted to hear, it was a lie. If you did say what you thought he wanted to hear and you were wrong, it was a beating. Lying and getting caught at it was the same result.

Like I said, you couldn't win.

CHAPTER SEVEN

"Wow, a whole day off, Barney! What would you like to do today, baby?"

The long-haired mutt lying beside her whuffled and pushed against her hand as Flak scratched behind his ears. The double bed was full of warm bodies, with the dog on one side and Andy the cat curled up at her spine.

She kept the air conditioning on super cold at night, but still woke in a sweat every morning from the animals' body heat. Welcome as it was in the drafty little house in the winter, she didn't have the heart to break them of the habit in the summertime.

Butting the cat over with her backside, she pushed Barney off the bed on the other side to free the blankets. He landed with a thump. Fifty solid pounds of hair and tongue, the collie-lab mix hopped back up in one bound, licking her and Andy—who swiped one clawless paw in protest. The cat's weaponry had been removed after Flak caught him on the curtains for the tenth time.

"Okay, guys, let's get moving." She darted in the bathroom down the hall from her bedroom. After a cursory wash, she used her damp hands to try to bring some order to the red curls running riot. As usual, she was unsuccessful. The only thing that kept them under control was a hat.

She reassured herself, as she had so many times, that it could be worse. The olive skin and hazel eyes looking back at her were better than the milk-white skin and freckles of the true redhead. She poked at the place where cheekbones should have been, but her face was still as rounded as she remembered it from the last time she'd looked in a mirror. At least she didn't have to scrub any makeup off. Sighing, she gave up and headed for the back door, tripping over Barney the whole way, and let him out.

He took off at a dead run the moment his paws hit the grass, and three squirrels scattered to their respective trees. One stayed eight feet up on a massive oak's trunk, cussing at the dog. Hard as Barney tried, his leaps fell a few inches short of the noisy rodent.

Flak shook her head and shut the door, heading for the coffee maker. She'd fallen in bed the night before too exhausted to set it up. Fighting the filters with sleep-numbed fingers, she finally coaxed one free from its brothers, and finished getting coffee made.

By that time, the insistent "rowrs" from the orange-striped tabby circling her feet grew too loud to ignore. "Okay, okay!" She grabbed the plastic jug of food from the top of the fridge and filled the bowl marked "Andy." The pottery dish was in its usual place, on the counter between the kitchen and breakfast nook. She'd long since resigned herself to the cat's counter-hopping habits, plus it kept Barney, the eating machine, out of the Meow Mix.

Shuffling into the flip-flops by the back door, she headed around the house and up the drive to get the newspaper. Still in her sleeping shorts and t-shirt, the fresh, early morning breeze played with the leg hairs she'd skipped shaving this week. It woke her enough to say a pleasant "Good morning" to Erma, who drove up just as she reached the road.

"Hey, lady, you're sure up early this morning." The mild sarcasm of her part-time housekeeper and pet sitter got a rise of Flak, whether it was intended or not.

"Oh hush, Erm—I been pulling double shifts for two weeks straight."

"Didn't Cliff get back from his honeymoon yet?" Flak pulled the Daily Sentinel from the bright yellow tube hung under her metal mailbox and stuck it under her arm.

"Yeah, Thursday. He's back at work tonight."

"Good! You need me this weekend?" The hopeful note in Erma's voice made Flak smile in spite of herself. Erma always needed the money, but never really wanted to do the work to get it. Housekeeper was kind of a charitable term for Erm, but the woman loved both of Flak's pets to death. It was well worth a few bucks every week to make sure the kids were okay.

"Nope—but if you can check on the boys again starting Monday, I'd appreciate it."

"No sweat. I gotta go—garage sales start at daylight, and I've already missed out on some good stuff."

"I'll leave a check out for you," Flak yelled after the truck. Erma waved an acknowledgment out the window.

Heading back down the rutted driveway, she smiled at the sight of her house sitting in its cleared space in the woods. Her election as sheriff two years before and the ensuing raise in pay meant she could quit renting, and it still thrilled her to realize this house was hers. The very dirt was hers, as were the frogs and lizards and spiders that populated the same. Made her grin every time she thought about it.

The smile swapped places with a frown at the sight of the filthy car with "Sheriff" in big black letters and the county seal painted on the door. Part of her day would have to be spent washing the dern car, which would mean a bath for the dog, because he couldn't resist the hose, which would mean a shower for her, because she'd be soaked, too.

"After my coffee," she muttered to herself. The burble and last throaty hiss sounded as she let herself in. The noise was barely louder than the purring cat, who remained over his bowl, eyes shut, front paws folded under.

"You happy now, bud?" She stroked his back on her way through. Andy opened one eye, and then resumed his blissful rumblings.

Barney butted his head against the back door, causing her to reflect that it wasn't actually correct that crossbreeds were smarter. She'd tried everything she could think of to teach him to bark at the door to go in and out, even read books on housetraining. Two years later, still no success.

She juggled her coffee and the newspaper to get a hand free and let him in. Placing everything on the brightly tiled breakfast table, she sat down with a sigh, sipped at the dark warmth in her cup, and flipped the newspaper open.

She read the *Sound Off* section first to see who was cranky today about how the county was being run. A quick look at the half-page of what passed for an entertainment section showed Ben Campbell was playing at the Caraban all week.

A dozen hours later, Flak stepped through the door of the Caraban Club, just outside the northern city limits. The remodeled, all-new Caraban Club, she noted.

A young man whose face she vaguely remembered leaned toward her over a waist-high counter. She'd long ago gotten used to the fact that half the people in or near Nacogdoches looked familiar. She couldn't shop at Wal-Mart without being stopped at least of dozen times. Sometimes, she even knew who they were. She nodded to him and kept walking.

"Whoa—hold it! I'm sorry, but are you a member?"

"Of what?" Then she realized what he meant. "No, I'm not, but I won't be drinking anyway."

"Uh-huh. Sorry, but you need a membership now to even go in—you know how the law is. Can't risk losing our license."

The weirdness of Texas' various laws on booze never ceased to amaze her. You could only serve alcohol in Nacogdoches County if you were at a private club, but private just meant you charged for membership. And you could buy membership for the night for a buck.

She ponied up her dollar and returned her wallet to her jeans' back pocket. The man handed her a card in return good for one night's membership.

Reading it, she walked on into the darker environs of the main bar. Glasses clinked, and the unharmonious smells of a crowd of people's breath, perfume, aftershave and smoke assaulted her. A glance at her watch confirmed the show wouldn't start for another twenty minutes.

"Hey darlin', watch where you're going." The collision startled her, but she stayed on her feet because the six-footer grabbed both her shoulders.

"I was," she said, and realized who had bumped into her. Even in the dim light, Ben's blond beard and toothy grin were unmistakable. Plus, he smelled good, too. "Hey, Ben, how are you?"

He looked at her, one eyebrow raised. "I seldom say this to a pretty girl, but I'm sorry, I don't think I know you."

"Flak Anders?" She wasn't sure why she'd made it a question.

He shook his head again, but seemed less sure.

"Anita Anders Barnes?" Again with the question. She knew who she was, what was wrong with her? "Curtis Lee's wife," she finally said, irritated with herself and with him.

"Oh my God—I'm sorry. You were in uniform the last time I saw you. I didn't recognize you in civvies. What the hell are you doing here?"

"Actually, I came here to see you. Got a minute?"

"For you? Sure. But I have to start my first set at nine, so there's not a whole lot of time."

"That's okay—let's sit down over there." She pointed at an empty table and chair near the rectangular raised platform with the band's equipment already set up.

A waitress appeared to take their drink orders, and departed with a knowing smirk. His head turned to watch the young woman walk away. He turned back. "You still a deputy?"

"Sheriff, now." Without meaning to, she pointed to where her badge usually hung on her left shirt pocket. She didn't wear civvies much these days—and had reminded herself as she was getting dressed that it was time to go buy a decent shirt or two. Couldn't stay in uniform twenty-four hours a day every day.

"Well, what brings the sheriff of Nacogdoches County out to a juke joint to see an old, broke-down, beat-up country singer?"

"Saw the ad in the paper that you were singing, just thought I'd drop by."

"For business or pleasure?" He cocked an eyebrow under the silver-banded, black felt cowboy hat, and she swallowed a tart remark the wrong way.

He thumped her on the back a little harder than she thought strictly necessary. She sipped the clear soda the waitress slid in front of her, gasped in a couple ragged breaths, grabbed the dinky napkin, and wiped a tear away.

"Hoo boy, I haven't got that much reaction from a good-looking woman in a long time. Choked you right up, huh?"

"Yeah." Flak's voice still rasped from the coughing fit, "But that's not why I'm here."

He shrugged. "I give up. Why are you here?"

She cleared her throat finally with a sharp cough. "Came to ask you a couple of questions about your daddy's death."

That eyebrow rose again, "If you're talking about Tucker Barnes, you must be misinformed. He was not my daddy. The name on the marquee is 'Campbell.'"

Flak snapped her fingers. "I knew that!" She looked toward the ceiling to help her memory along. "Yeah, your mama told me once you and Frederick were from earlier marriages than Curt and the girls."

"Mama used to call us all a bunch of serial marriers," with a grin, "But we got it honest. Her daddy was married like twelve times, she was married four. I'm happily divorced from my third, and you're my little brother's what? Fourth wife?"

"Fifth," Flak said dryly, "But I'm not here to talk about marriage. Sounds like you and Tucker didn't get along so well."

"You are absolutely correct, Sheriff." He took a drink from the beer in front of him. "In fact, that's the understatement of the century."

"Did Tucker raise you?"

"Mama raised us," Ben corrected her. "Tucker showed up nights and weekends to beat the hell out of us and work us into the ground."

"So you hated him?"

"You could say that." Those green eyes shone like a cat's, even in the dim lights of the showroom. She had a suspicion, if he was capable of it, his ears would be laid back.

"You are an amazing bunch, you know? Every

one of you kids hated him, and none of you shy from saying it." She sipped from her soda again.

"Actually, that ain't quite true, Sheriff. One of us didn't hate him," Ben said, but as he opened his mouth to finish the thought, the drummer ka-botta-botta-boomed on the stage. "I gotta get my mike checks done. I'll talk to you after the first set."

She hadn't planned to stay for the music, but ended up enjoying it. The four-piece band backing Ben sounded good, even if they were a little too loud for the small venue. They covered a number of Hank Williams Jr.'s tunes, interspersed with Brooks and Dunn, Trace Adkins and Toby Keith. Ben's energy and smile were infectious, and she found herself tapping a foot without meaning to. The crowd swelled, and he often took his cordless microphone down and sang from the middle of the dancers.

A number of women guests whispered behind their hands or full glasses, and glared at her. She figured she must be at the "girlfriend" table and ignored them.

Problem was, as usual, half of the faces belonged to people she knew, if only by sight. She assumed the rumor of her dating her husband's brother would beat her back to town.

His first set finished, Ben yelled at her, "Order me a beer, would you honey?" and disappeared toward the bathroom.

She sighed and raised his half-full bottle toward the waitress, who nodded.

Not long after, she felt a hand stroke the back of her hair, and Ben came past her.

"Damn it, you're making a spectacle! All these people think we're together!" she hissed at him as he sat down. He bolted the rest of the warm beer, and then took a sip of the cold one.

"Screw 'em," he said succinctly. "Small town, small minds."

"Besides, maybe it'll improve your standing when they realize you've moved on to the better-looking brother," he said louder, gazing over her left shoulder.

"Oh, crap." She knew exactly who Ben was talking to, and it definitely wasn't her.

"Hey, Neets," a familiar male voice said behind her, and a hand landed on each shoulder.

"Hello, asshole," Curt continued, but this time to Ben. She could feel the fingers of his left hand tightening on her shoulder, and the other stiffly pressed down, fingers jutting toward his half-brother.

Ben smirked. "Hello, little brother. I didn't see you standing there."

"Well, why don't you walk outside and let me kick the crap out of you, big brother? Then you'll know I'm really here." The pressure on her left shoulder tightened.

"Much as I would love it, I wouldn't want to bruise my knuckles on your hard head. I have to hold a mike here in a minute." Ben took a sip from his beer, but Flak noticed he never took his eyes off Curt. She wasn't sure whether to look up at Curtis, or if she would just be poking the bear.

Though the noise level hadn't dropped, the swiveled heads surrounding them made Flak aware of the attention centered on the table.

"Why don't you and I take this outside, Curt?" She regretted her choice of words as soon as Ben snickered.

Those green eyes were even more catlike when he was being sarcastic. "Yeah, why don't you let your wife take care of you, boy?"

Flak ducked out from under Curt's bad hand, coming up to stand beside him. "Why don't you just shut up, Ben and get back on the stage."

Laughing, he stood and shoved his chair back with his knees. Onstage, he said something to the band she couldn't catch. The music started.

She grabbed Curt's arm. With his fist clenched at pocket level, it felt like trying to move a steel pipe buried in concrete.

What was she was going to do if he wouldn't go with her? She was just trying to decide, as the opening bars of "Statue of a Fool," segued into the verse, and his arm relaxed. He shrugged off her hand and headed toward the door.

She struggled to keep up with his long strides.

Outside, her boots struck a higher, faster note on the pavement than his as he headed for his truck. He reached for the door handle.

Desperate to stop him before he left, "Stop. Please. I need to ask you something."

Facing her, he crossed his arms and settled into the "I'm waiting" stance she remembered far too well.

Legs spread, weight far back on his heels, the pearl snaps on his starched white shirt glowed in the light thrown by the street lamp at the city limit sign.

His bull rider-style straw cowboy hat cast a shadow over his face, but the expression was clear in her memory.

Flak reached over Curt's crossed arms into his shirt pocket and fished out his Marlboro reds and lighter. She lit one, careful not to inhale, and handed it to him filter first.

He reached out slowly, took it between the ring and little fingers of his damaged right hand, and then brought it to his lips.

When he blew out the smoke, the tension in the air blew out along with it. He leaned against the truck as if too tired to stand unsupported.

"Damn it, Neets, what the hell were you doing here with him?"

"Get off your high horse, bubba. It wasn't like he made it look."

"Yeah?" Curt kept his head down, maybe to hide his emotions under his hat brim.

Flak tucked the lighter and cigarettes back into his shirt pocket and gentled her voice. "Yeah. I was just asking him questions about your dad."

"So you're on the job, huh? Where's your badge?"

"In my pocket. Believe me; your brother does nothing for me." She smiled at him, but he still wasn't looking at her.

"Half-brother."

"You know, that's the first time I've heard any of you use 'half.'"

"Mmm," he said through another drag of the fast-disappearing cigarette. "Mama didn't raise us to think that way. But she's dead."

"I remember."

"Do you?" He took his hat off with one hand, pushed the thick shock of still-black hair back with the other, and then reset it further back. The physical shadow disappeared from his face, but other shadows remained.

"Do you really? Do you remember I lost you both inside of six months? Do you…" Whatever he'd been about to say, he must have thought better. "Aw, to hell with this, it's old news. What did you want to ask me?"

"Oh. Yeah." With an effort, Flak got her mind back on track.

"When I talked to you the night your dad…died, you said everyone in the family hated him. But Ben just told me all but one of you did. What did he mean?"

"Huh. He was probably talking about Frederick. He was kind of the golden boy when we were growing up." He looked at the cigarette butt in his hand as if it were a bug, and then flicked it toward the road.

"So Fred got along with Tucker?"

"Yeah, I guess. If he didn't, he never said. He was the football hero, married right out of high school, and had a bunch of blonde babies. You remember him—he lived right next door to Mama."

"Preacher man?" She hazarded the guess—a bulky man was all she remembered, quiet most of the time.

He barked a laugh. "Yeah, you're right. His wife pushed him into starting a church when you and I were together. Didn't last, but he's still a God-shouter."

He lit another cigarette.

"What does it matter? If you're still on about somebody murdering Daddy, Frederick's the least likely one. He takes 'Thou shalt not kill,' more to heart than the rest of us do."

"You are a wild bunch." She shook her head.

"Yeah, we put the 'fun' in dysfunctional, don't we?"

Another drag, and then, "I gotta go, Neets. You need a ride?"

She shook her head. "My cruiser's parked out back—didn't want to scare off the customers."

He got in the truck and rolled down the window. "Thanks."

Surprised, she asked, "For what?"

"For keeping me from kicking his scrawny ass. Mama wouldn't have liked it."

"Um. You're welcome." She returned his smile.

He gunned the rumbly motor to life and pulled onto Highway 59 headed south.

Flak watched the truck disappear. It was the smile that always killed her.

She could handle anything Curt threw at her from the anger and dismay side of the wall, but when he smiled, she still had to take a breath.

She shook her head at her own stupidity and walked back into the club. After showing her membership card to the over-decorated young woman now sitting behind the counter, she inched through the crowd on the dance floor and resumed her seat.

Engrossed in thought, she didn't notice the set was over until Ben turned his chair around and sat down on it backwards. One arm balanced along the chair's back, and the other reached out for his warm-again beer.

"Ah, it's thirsty work," he said and waved the empty at the waitress. "Thanks for getting rid of that feisty little bastard. So now, it's just the two of us again?"

"Where were you on the night of the fifteenth?"

"Okay, then." Ben let out a philosophical sigh. "Looks like the woman disappeared in the parking lot and the sheriff took her place." He took a long swallow from the new longneck bottle the waitress placed in front of him.

Flak asked him again, but kept the question mild. "So, where were you?"

"Let's see…the fifteenth… we were playing at the State Pen."

"In Huntsville?"

"Nope. It's this little juke joint in Beaumont. Opened up in June, trying to get some business. They hired us for a week-long gig. Forty drunks and my band enough of an alibi for you?"

She nodded, "As soon as I check it out, it will be."

Ben leaned forward, crossing both arms along the back of the chair in between them. "So, just out of curiosity, does my little brother have an alibi?"

"You'll have to ask him." Flak hated to admit it, even to herself, but she liked being able to avoid the question—she'd dealt with them so long she was starting to talk like them.

"Huh. Did he tell you Tucker tried to kill him?" The hopeful rise at the end of the question told Flak the man would be more than happy to cause his little brother some trouble.

"Maggie told me about it." Flak couldn't help the satisfaction coloring her answer.

"Well, you have been a busy little sheriff, haven't you? Did she also tell you about Curtis Lee's fantasy about killing Tucker?" The snide note in Ben's voice was getting to be more than a little irritating.

"No, but Jenny said you talked about killing him, too."

"Yeah, the night of Mama's funeral. I think all of us except Frederick were in on the conversation. No, he was there, too. Of course, it might just be a coincidence that Curtis Lee was the only one of us wanted to set him on fire." He cocked an eyebrow again. She nodded for him to keep going.

"The old man still lived in a camper on the back of the old Ford pickup he had before he wrecked it. Curtis Lee said he wanted to block the door of the camper with his own pickup truck, and then set it on fire. He said he wanted to hear him screaming and beating on the door while he roasted alive."

CHAPTER EIGHT

Jenny

Mama was so careful to keep his morning routine exactly like he demanded it. One wrong word, or being too slow with his cigars, whatever, and she had ruined his whole day. He came home in a good mood that day—something must have gone right.

The week before, something got screwed up one morning, and he was already boiling by the time he went out to the truck. You have to realize, some of this, Mama and me and my sister figured out later. It was like we went over and over this stuff trying to see if we could have done something different and fixed it. Anyway, either he threw his thermos in the truck when he left, or he dropped it at some later point in the morning and broke the glass inside. Later, he accuses my mother of putting ground glass in his coffee.

With time to work up a head of steam, he hit even harder than usual.

But that was the week before.

On this particular day, he was happy and decided it was music time. After supper he pulled out the Bell and Howell reel-to-reel and his guitar. Between tuning the guitar and fiddling with the tape player, he told stories about playing in the honky-tonks, behind chicken wire to avoid the inevitable "who can hit the lead singer in the head with a beer bottle" contest.

He told my sis and me to sing the song we were assigned to learn during his last good mood. We were happy to sing for him, but wary, too—who knows when the other guy living inside him would pop out and beat the snot out of us.

He fiddled with the buttons on the tape player and then made us sing while he played the guitar and recorded us, over and over again. He told us what we did wrong.

"Don't move, just sing."

He grabbed us each by the waist and showed us where our diaphragms are.

"Sing from here! Enunciate clearly. Don't say can't—no one in this family is allowed to say can't. You know how to do this, I've taught you enough times."

The boys escaped that session. They didn't usually, but you know how kids always assume someone is getting something more than they're getting? They have this overdeveloped sense of fairness.

Well, it was the other way around for all of us. Each of us had all we could take. We wanted less. The boys seemed to escape most of him. Between sports and just being male, they had some protection we didn't.

We could hear our brothers playing outside as darkness fell. Whatever mutiny we had in our hearts, we didn't let it show on our faces. So we sang and sang and sang.

Mama was in the kitchen singing too, a soprano echo of the song we'd just finished for the tenth time.

It was one of the good days.

CHAPTER NINE

Flak sipped her black coffee and made a face. Her third cup of the morning still hadn't made a dent in her end-of-week, tired-out, why-did-I-run-for-this-job-anyway blahs.

A deputy walked past her door, and before she could get too far, Flak asked, "Hey, Harley, you made any progress on those background checks yet?"

The very large woman put it in reverse and backed up to the doorway.

"Yes, ma'am, I've got some of it—I'm waiting on a callback on one of them."

"What you got so far?"

"Well, for one thing, I searched everywhere, and haven't found divorce papers for you and Curtis Lee yet."

Flak felt the muscles of her face tighten up and held back the explosion lurking just under the surface. "I'm well aware I'm still married. Where exactly were you looking to find this out?"

"Well, I didn't know it was a secret or nothing." The sullen note in the deputy's voice reminded Flak it wasn't Harley's fault she'd never gotten around to divorcing Curt.

"Don't worry about it—but don't be spreading it around."

"Ain't none of my business." Harley shrugged, creating a ripple spreading all the way down to tree-trunk thighs encased in strained khaki fabric.

"What else you got?" The phone on the desk rang as the deputy opened her mouth.

"Give me a minute, will you?" Flak motioned her away. Harley quit blocking the light from the hallway, and she answered on the second ring.

"Sheriff."

"Hey, Flak, it's Jim."

Flak couldn't figure out if she was happy or not the fire inspector was calling back this quick. She knew from the last phone call it would take them a while to get any results. "Hey, man, how're things in Houston town?" She forced cheer into her voice.

"Oh, fair to middlin', but I might have something for you on the Barnes fire." The voice went on without giving her time to react. "I know it took us a while, and I'm sorry, but everybody got called out on the ship fire in the Channel."

Flak resisted the urge to tell him to get on with it. "Yeah, I heard about it. Everybody okay?"

"All our bunch are, but thank the good Lord we don't have to clean up the mess."

"So what you got on my fire?"

"Well, you know I told you the accelerant didn't come up on our database. We expanded our search, did some poking around, and at least got some of it nailed down."

Flak bit her lip to keep from urging him on.

"It just wasn't the kind of stuff we usually find in arson. That's the other reason it took a while."

Flak limited herself to another, "Uh-huh."

"It appears to be some kind of rocket or missile fuel. Like I said, it's new, at least in this combination. And we know now it was in a glass container. Some of the samples I brought back didn't match the rest of the glass in the house and showed the strongest traces of this accelerant."

"So somebody brought it there?"

"Well, I can't come up with any good reason why an old man would have a glass full of rocket fuel in the house."

"You got a point."

"I ain't closed the books on it yet, but I'm officially ruling it arson. You got any information from your investigation might help us pinpoint a manufacturer? It would sure help lighten the research load."

"No, but I should know more here shortly. I'll call you." Flak was eager to get off the phone, but his next words brought her up short.

"Oh—before I forget—did y'all come up with any bullets on the scene?"

"Yeah—we found a .22 rifle under the bed, and some casings and bullets. We figured they'd been set off by the heat of the fire." Flak sat back in her chair, wondering where he was going with this.

"Maybe so. But one fragment we got from the fuel container has a circular chip, like a bullet impacted the glass."

"I don't get it."

"Some of these high-tech fuels combust or explode on exposure to oxygen. Preliminary theory is somebody busted in the bathroom window, set this container on the sill inside, and then shot at it from a distance to set it off. Fit's the evidence we've got so far, but it's still just a theory; I can't prove it yet."

"So I'm looking for a shooter who can get their hands on rocket fuel?" Flak couldn't help the disbelief in her voice.

"I'd say so—and it wouldn't have to be a big container. From the curve of the glass samples, I'm figuring about the size of a soft drink can."

"That ain't much fuel to start a fire."

"Doesn't have to be with something this volatile."

Harley loomed once more in the doorway.

"Thanks, Jim—I'll call you." Flak hung up and motioned the large woman to a chair. "What have you got for me Harl?"

"Short version or long?"

"Short for now. I'll read your report later."

Harley grimaced. Flak was well aware the deputy hated typing. Getting those sausage-size fingers to fit on a keyboard must be pure torture.

"Okay. Right now, it looks like we've got an oilman, a singing trucker, a painter, a consultant and a baby-making whack job."

Flak leaned back in her chair and breathed in a scent mixed of coffee, a whiff of old urine from the jail down the hall, and the unexpectedly girlish floral perfume Harley wore. "Maybe a little longer than that."

The deputy picked up the clipboard she'd rested on the desk and shifted uneasily in the too-small chair. Her knees bumped Flak's desk with a muffled metallic thump with every move.

"In order from the oldest—Benjamin Calhoun Campbell, forty-nine years of age, oldest son of Emlyn Jones Campbell Miller Barnes. Birth father's long dead. Drives a gas tanker all over East Texas, sings in honkytonks around South and East Texas at night. Married and divorced three times, has six kids."

"Really? Six?"

"Yeah—all grown and scattered from Nebraska to Houston." Harley paused.

"Okay, next." Flak found it hard to imagine Ben as a father figure to anybody. Slimy jerk.

"Frederick Anthony Miller, forty-seven years old, his daddy died when he was two months old. Works for Garrison Oil; been with 'em since God was a baby, like twenty-three years or more. Spends a month out and around inspecting oil and refining facilities all over Louisiana, Texas and offshore, then he spends a month at home. Active in his local church, married right out of high school, two kids, both married and living in the area."

"Sounds like a boy scout to me. He doesn't have a record?"

Harley paged back and forth a few seconds on the clipboard. "Lots of speeding tickets, but he's paid 'em all. You want me to keep going?"

Flak nodded.

"Okay, well, next is Curtis Lee Barnes, forty-five, painter, married five times, divorced four." Harley kept her eyes glued to the papers in her hand.

"And?" Flak prompted.

"That's pretty much it. You know about his daddy's death. Couple of bar fights and tickets, but he must stay under the radar most of the time. If he's even got a bank account, I couldn't find it."

"Okay—then there's just the girls."

"Oldest girl is Maggie Lynn Barnes Kovax, 43, married to a retired Air Force fella. Address is a Dallas suburb."

"She still married to him?"

"No divorces on record. They married while she was in the Air Force in 1980. She got out, he went career. She got her degree, with honors. Is summa cum laude the best one? I can never remember."

"Yes," Flak said, lost in thought, trying to process everything.

"Last known employment…" Harley flipped back and forth once more on the clipboard "was consulting for a big defense company in Dallas. Let's see… they're called Kindjal Industries."

"Consulting about what?" Flak asked.

"Haven't gotten ahold of that—still waiting on a phone call."

"What does Kindjal make?"

"Says here," Harley flipped through the papers again, "Weapons for the military."

"What kind?"

"Doesn't say."

"Okay—how about Jenny?"

"Jennifer Andrea Barnes Samuels, forty-one, divorced in early 2000, four kids, the youngest is five years old, and all the kids are with her ex-husband in California. She's been in and out of state mental hospitals since '99, which was how he got custody. Suicide attempt put her in the first time. No present address."

"Change to present address Looneyville—that's where she and Maggie are now. I wonder why

Maggie's here instead of Dallas." Flak was looking straight at Harley, but her mind was about eighteen miles away.

The deputy shrugged again, and made a note.

With a mental jerk, Flak brought herself back to the office and the task in front of her. Well, the task she was going to give out, anyway.

"Okay, Harley, there are a few more bits we need to fill in the gaps. Get more on Kindjal Industries and what Maggie did for them. We're looking to find out whether they make rockets or missiles, and if she was in research and development. Particularly fuel research and development."

Flak sat forward and pushed enough paper aside to put her elbows on her desk. "Also, find out whether any of the facilities Frederick visits are labs for creating missile or rocket fuels. And find out whether the company Ben drives for has any association with the same stuff." She thought hard for a moment.

"I need the exact date of Emlyn Barnes' death. And also, if any of the five are hunters or shooters and whether they own a .22 rifle or pistol."

Harley's big old hand was moving a mile a minute on the clipboard as she scribbled down the instructions. "Anything else?"

"Check on Tucker Barnes' history, see if we ever arrested him for anything."

"Yes, ma'am." Harley stood up and maneuvered her bulk through the constricted space to the door.

"Oh—and keep the rocket and missile side of it quiet, okay?"

"You got it, boss." The deputy popped out of the doorway like a cork departing a wine bottle.

The phone jolted Flak out of her reverie, and she answered it with a sigh.

"Sheriff."

"Hey girl," came Garvey's bass rumble.

"Hey, Garv. What's going on?" The cheeriness wasn't such an effort this time.

"Oh, not much. I just thought I'd see if you was up for dinner and a movie tonight."

"I don't think I have enough patience for a movie, but I'll take you up on dinner. Actually, why don't you come out to the house, and I'll cook." A long pause descended, and she started getting a little hot about it.

Finally, Garvey responded. "Well, considering the fact I ain't quite got over the last time you cooked for me, why don't I just pick something out and bring it with me." You could hear the smile in his voice even over the phone.

"I'm a good cook!"

"Mary was a good cook." Garvey referred to his wife, a good friend of Flak's, who had died five years before of breast cancer. "You, on the other hand, are more of 'the smoke alarm's going off, dinner must be done,' school of cookery."

"I swear, Garv, that really was a blackened fish recipe." She couldn't help returning the long-distance grin. It was one of her more memorable foul-ups in the kitchen.

"I understand that, and I believe you, but the Cajuns did not mean the fish was supposed to be black all the way through—you're supposed to leave some white in the middle."

Flak laughed. "Kiss my ass, Chief Garvey!"

"I'll kiss anything you want me to kiss, ma'am, but it'll have to be later—how's seven?"

"Eight o'clock would be better—I got a boatload of end-of-month paperwork to get caught up." She riffled through the papers on her desk with yet another sigh. Had to stop doing that, she was starting to sound like a leaky tire.

"Sounds good to me."

"Oh, by the way, we got a preliminary arson determination from Jim on the Barnes fire on Appleby-Sand."

"No surprise. You got a suspect?"

"Lord help me, Garv, I've got a whole passel of 'em. You got any firebugs might fit this as a pattern?"

"No—the only similarities are between this one and the Looneyville store back in May. It didn't cause near as much damage."

"What similarities were there?" Her hopes started to rise.

"Oh, mainly just the window being busted in. We figured it was just a kids' prank, if I remember correctly."

She shook her head, even though she knew he couldn't see her. "I was really hoping for something out of that, but I don't imagine a broken window is enough to tie anything together. Got one last question for you about the Barnes fire, though— were there gas lines going in the house?"

Garvey snorted. "You know—I meant to talk to you about it, because it didn't make any sense at all. Maybe you ought to ask Curtis Lee."

Not at all what she wanted to do at the moment. "Ask him what?"

"There was a butane tank, away from the house in the trees, real hard to see. I sent Randy to turn it off first thing. He said it was already turned off at the tank when he got there. I told Jim about it, meant to mention it to you. Since it couldn't be the cause of the fire, I didn't put it in my report." Garvey's voice sounded worried.

"Don't sweat it too much, man. I'll send somebody out there to print it."

"Okay and I'll have Randy run over there for comparison prints so you can knock his out."

A sigh on the other end of the phone—sounded like he'd caught her habit. "Much obliged, Chief."

His voice brightened. "So I'll see you tonight... You want anything in particular?"

"No, surprise me."

Harley stuck her head back around the door. For a big gal, she sure moved soft. Flak said goodbye to Garvey and hung up.

"Hey, boss—I got a date for you. Emlyn Barnes died July 16, 1999."

Flak nodded grimly. "That was the same month and day of the Barnes fire."

"Which one of 'em you think did it?"

"Dang it, Harley, I'm not sure any of 'em did it! I'm just trying to get all our ducks in a row. Speaking of which, as soon as you can, look through those .22 bullets we recovered from the scene and see if you can find one shows signs of rifling, like it was fired."

"Yes, ma'am. Anything else?"

"Yeah, and then I'll leave you to get on with it. Would you please send Ed out to the Barnes place and have him fingerprint the butane tank? Tell him Randy will come over from the fire station to give him a set of comparison prints."

Harley blinked at Flak and then stared down at her size twelve boots. "The only prints we got for any of the Barnes bunch are Curtis Lee's, from the bar fight booking."

"I know," Flak said with a sigh, and started shoving papers around on her desk. "I know."

About four hours later, the sheriff discreetly burped behind her hand as she led the way to the lawn chairs parked under the oak tree. "That was great, Garv—thanks,"

"No sweat, girl. Lots easier to pick up some Tex-Mex than be taking the pink stuff all night long." Garvey leaned back in the webbed frame and stretched his long legs out, one booted ankle over the other.

"You busting on my cooking again?" Flak took her own seat on the other side of the patio table. She discreetly loosened the top button of her uniform pants. She'd have to start running again—but exercise time was tough to find these days.

"Yeah, I reckon I was." He pulled a tobacco pouch and scruffy pipe from his shirt pocket.

"I am just too tired to get up and smack you for your sass." She leaned her head back in the chair and crossed her booted feet at the ankles.

"I appreciate it—I'd hate to have to turn you over my knee," Garvey said.

Flak observed a calm silence as he finished the complicated assembly and ceremonious ignition of the tobacco. The pipe smoke drifted over to her, barely visible in the light of the nearby bug zapper. The smell reminded her of the way her dad always smelled—leather and smoke.

Her peaceful memories were interrupted by a loud rustle. She straightened and looked behind her. The dense trees at her property line were a massive wall in the darkness.

"It's just your dang dog," Garvey said. "Chasing an armadillo, most likely. Mutt ain't got two brain cells to rub together."

She settled back in her chair. "Aw, Barney's okay. Smarter than some the men I used to date."

"Huh," Garv snorted. "Yeah, I'd say your partner picker is pretty much broke."

"Maybe. But at least I done some picking. Did you ever go out with anybody but Mary?" She had known Mary long before she met Garvey—and was curious about the man's history.

Since Mary's death, they had slowly been getting to know each other without his wife and her best friend to serve as mediator, but she couldn't remember this coming up before.

The fire chief nodded. "A few. Before I met her. I told you I went out with Maggie Barnes a couple times."

Flak relaxed further into her chair. "Mary wouldn't have wanted you to just keep on grieving, you know."

"I know. But the only woman I'd consider dating is married."

"Do I know her?"

"Yeah, I reckon you do," he muttered, and fished out his lighter to get his pipe going again.

Flak figured she'd best leave that one alone.

After puffing his pipe alight once more. "Ah, speaking of that subject, you ever going to divorce Curtis Lee?"

"Weeelll, I was kind of waiting on him to divorce me."

"For four years?"

"Four and a half, actually."

"You know, I was still wandering around missing Mary when Miz Emlyn died and y'all fell apart. Couldn't see a foot past my own nose. What happened to you and Curt, anyway?"

Flak straightened up a bit in the chair, crossed her legs at the knee. "Oh hell, I don't know. It was right after a whacked-out Christmas at his mama's house. I'd missed them the other two years we'd been married 'because I was working, but I made a special effort to get time off that year." Flak was silent for a few moments, remembering.

"You know, I loved Miz Emlyn. She had the best sense of humor. She gave out the horse's butt of the year award every Christmas to whichever family member showed their ass the most."

"Really?"

"Swear—it was the back end of a horse tacked on a little wood base. Somebody got it every stinking year, too." Flak smiled, remembering.

"Something happen in particular to you and Curt?"

"No. Or at least not so's I remember. We just got in another fight on the way home. He said I was trying to cut his balls off, playing deputy. I told him I wasn't playing. It was the beginning of a fight that kept going for weeks. I think we just… both wore out. He left in January."

"You still love him?"

Flak had to think on that one a minute. Her silence lasted long enough for three bugs to commit suicide, each with a harsh buzz and crackle from the zapper. "I don't know."

More bugs died as Garvey laboriously relit his pipe. Flak realized it was not the answer he'd been expecting, but then she hadn't known herself until it came out of her mouth.

"Well, I guess I'll get going." Garvey levered his lanky frame from the lawn chair's grasp, pipe clenched in his teeth, with a grunt.

She pushed herself out of her own chair with an effort. "Yeah—I gotta get inside and call Dorrie. Have to remind her to send somebody to pick up Jasper Jay. It's payday at the plant."

Garvey shook his head. "Faith-Ann's going to kill him someday."

"I don't think so. The worst she's ever done was break his arm."

"No, the worst she's ever done was marry a man thinking she could change him." The pair strolled toward the back of the house.

"You know what they say, bubba. A man marries a woman, and a woman marries the man she thinks he can be." Flak mounted the short set of stairs, bringing her to Garvey's eye level.

"Is that what you did with Curtis Lee?" Garvey tapped his pipe on the side of the house and carefully ground ember and ash into the grass.

"Actually, I think it was the other way around. I'm pretty sure Curt thought, somewhere under this uniform beat the heart of a girly kind of girl. He didn't like what he actually found."

Garvey looked her straight in the eye. "Then he was an idiot."

She shook her head. "We both were pretty dang stupid."

"Well, it's nice to see you haven't changed, anyway."

"That's enough out of you for one night, buddy boy. Go home." Flak grinned to take the sting out of the dismissal.

"Yeah. See you next week." He headed around the side of his house toward his truck.

She opened the screen door and walked into the kitchen. Barely two steps in, Barney hit her in the stomach with both paws. She grunted from the impact, "Get down, boy." She dropped into a kitchen chair and let him rear up, paws in her lap.

Holding on to both his ears to keep his tongue out of her face, she crooned, "So it wasn't you chasing armadillos, huh? We must have some kind of critter out there. Maybe a deer or something. Why don't you go out and run 'em off for me, baby."

At the word "out." Barney's ears went up and his tail began whipping the table leg into submission.

His rear paws jitterbugged as he jumped from one side to the other. His claws sounded like castanets on the tile.

Flak let him out and watched him head for the woods. For once, he ran without a sound. She shut both doors and headed for the phone to call Dorrie. She knew Barney would butt his head up against the door when he was ready to come back in the house for the night.

CHAPTER TEN
Jenny

It was the only time I ever actually saw my father cry. Or maybe I should say ever saw a tear in his eye.

First—you have to understand how poor we really were. I didn't understand at the time, but I can see it looking back. We never took animals to the veterinarian. Ever. No shots, no nothing. I hear you can buy health insurance now for your pets—well, if there was such a thing even for people then, we hadn't heard of it. Now there was life insurance, but I only knew because my father brought it up every time he decided my mother was plotting his murder in order to get the money.

Anyway, if an animal got mortally sick or too old to make it, the only thing we could do was try home remedies on it, and then put a bullet through its head as a gesture of mercy.

One of the few times we must have had a little cash, my father purchased a purebred German shepherd. He had some grand notion of breeding her for profit, I'm sure, plus he wanted a guard dog, even though we owned nothing worth protecting at the time.

So, we kids basically grew up with this dog. It didn't all work out like my father planned. In hindsight, none of his wonderful ideas panned out like he thought they would. Maybe that's why he was such a mean bastard.

One of the ways the dog didn't work out was, every spring, her fur would fall out from her ribcage clear back to the end of her tail. And she was a big dog. So here's all this dark grey skin, and a naked tail bone on the back end of a beautiful front end. My father decided she was allergic to grass, so he had Mama bathe her in everything from oatmeal to baking soda. Now, you could probably take her to a vet and get her a shot, but like I said, we couldn't have afforded it even if it had crossed our minds.

Over the years, none of the remedies worked, so for the winter months, we had a gorgeous German shepherd, and every spring, we ended up with a half-rat, half dog wandering around the yard.

Queenie threw a litter of half-breed pups from the neighborhood mutt every spring, too, usually coinciding with the time all her hair fell out. Mama's pet theory was the dog was allergic to having children. Of course, she'd come up with this whenever we were at our most aggravating.

The other way the dog didn't work out the way Daddy planned was that, while she was certainly protective, she was most protective about his children. He had to tie her up every time he decided to beat on us unless he wanted to get his head ripped off by a hundred pounds or so of snarling, half-naked guard dog. We were pretty bright kids, so every time he headed for Queenie with a rope, we'd head for the woods.

Actually, from this vantage point, I guess every time we ever had animals, they were the fallout from some grand money-making scheme of his. We kids had to feed calves one spring with these huge bottles, which was kind of fun. He bought tons of feed and stuff for them, and sold them as soon as they were grown to the dairy farmer down the road at a loss.

We dealt with incubators and baby chicks and building a chicken pen and a chicken house so we could sell eggs, which never happened. He bought the pigs before he built the pen, so we gave up the living room to them for a few weeks while he and the boys built the pen. Mama had me and my sis scrubbing the living room for weeks after the pigs got their new house.

Of course, once we got them installed in their new living quarters, the pigs' main aim was escape, so we were constantly running after them. When they were full grown, all three of them escaped. We retrieved two of them, but the third one went feral.

Well, the thought of losing control over something he owned drove my father right out of his tree.

Now, this man was an amazing shot. I've seen him take the head off a coral snake from thirty yards away with a rifle. He decided he could "crease" the pig, by laying a shot right across the front of her skull with the thirty-ought-six, and it wouldn't kill her, it would just knock her out.

He actually did crease her, but it was a little deep. We ate a lot of pork for the next couple of months, which would have been fine, if the pig hadn't been named for my mother's sister. There was an awful lot of packages labeled "Aunt Robbie" in the freezer.

The gun was the same one he used on Queenie when she took ill. She had suffered for weeks, to the point where she was dragging her hindquarters around behind her. Mama finally convinced him he had to put the dog out of her misery.

Like I said, it was the only tear I ever saw him shed. You'd think it would make me feel better about him. But the honest truth is, I don't believe he would have shed even one tear about shooting one of his children. I don't believe he would have cared about that at all.

CHAPTER ELEVEN

Flak stood on the sunshine-warmed stoop in her sleeping shorts and t-shirt, and shouted for the dog. "Barney, here boy."

She jumped and turned when the man came around the corner of the house, frantically patting her right hip for a gun that wasn't there.

"Crap, Curt, you scared the be-Jesus out of me."

"Sorry—I just heard you yelling back here and figured I'd come around. Who's Barney?"

"My dog." She eyed him critically. "You not working today?"

"Promised Mags I'd go out and paint the store for her. She said you'd been out there."

"I didn't hear you pull up."

"Yeah, I figured." He grinned. "I put a new muffler on Betsy just so I could sneak up on the local womenfolk. Hate seeing them scatter like rats."

"Yeah, right. More like so you can sneak out after and not get caught."

He frowned at her. "Why don't you go get a cup of coffee. You're much more sociable with caffeine in you. I'll go look for the damned dog."

Flak glared at him and turned to go inside.

"You might want to put a bra on while you're at it," he said as he strode for the tree line.

"I hope he bites you right on the ass," Flak said in conversational tones as she pulled open the screen door.

"Heard that!"

"Meant you to!" She stomped inside the house, poured a cup and looked at it a second, then headed for her bedroom to get dressed.

Bra, panties, fairly clean t-shirt and jeans later, she grabbed the mug and bolted half of it. Still barefoot, she sat down on the back steps.

Curt emerged from the tree line and ambled up to her. "He's probably chasing a deer or something. He'll come back when he gets hungry."

"He never stayed out all night before."

"He might have just found some gal in heat and be out there having a good time."

"You *would* think that. I had him neutered."

"It just takes away the follow-through, not the interest."

She stared at the wall of pines and hardwoods, willing the mutt to show his shaggy face.

"Look—why don't you leave some food out on the step here, and come with me to the store?"

"Whatever for? And besides, y'all are all part of an ongoing investigation." She continued to scour her surroundings for any sign of her goofy dog.

"You still think somebody killed Daddy?"

"Yep."

"Well, then, think of it as more investigation time. Mags said Frederick's coming out later, and Ben's even honoring us with his presence."

"You two kiss and make up?"

"Let's just say we called a temporary truce."

She shook her head. "I don't know, Curt. I'm not sure it's a good idea."

He put both hands on his hips, and drawled, "Well, I'll tell you what, little lady, we'll let you take Frederick out back and pistol whip him until he confesses, how's that?"

She smiled at him, but was struck by an idea before she could respond to his silliness. "Why don't y'all shorten his name? Everybody else in the family has a nickname except you."

He shrugged. "Never thought about it much."

"Does Maggie know you're asking me?"

"Good God, woman, you're like a grasshopper this morning. How much coffee did you drink in the last five minutes? Maggie won't care."

"Don't be so sure." Flak thought for a few seconds. It might just be a chance to talk to all of them in one place and see how they reacted to each other. "Okay, I'll go—but you have to bring me back home the minute I'm ready to come back; doesn't matter if it's only ten minutes after we get there."

"I swear. Your chariot awaits, madam," and he motioned around the side of the house.

She laughed and stood. "Let me get some shoes on and put some food out for Barney and Andy." At Curt's lifted eyebrow, she said, "Andy's my cat. And I have to call in to the office and check on Jasper Jay."

"They took him home just as I left to come over here."

"Now, how the hell would you know that?"

"Police band radio—don't you have one?"

Flak just looked at him.

"Um, I'll be in the truck."

Walking around the house, Flak marveled that Curt's old rust bucket truck still ran at all. Two of the four letters on the tailgate had either rusted off or been painted over, so now it just said OD. She took a peek in the bed, and it was stained with layer after layer of paint, or at least what could be seen of it. A short ladder and boxes full of paint tools covered part of it.

Flak's awkward maneuver to get herself and her coffee into the truck left her pulling her t-shirt back into place, but not before Curt saw the leather holster at the small of her back.

"You do know I was joking about you pistol-whipping Frederick, right?" He put the truck in gear as he spoke. The rutted driveway shook the whole frame of the rusted-out wreck, and Flak scrabbled for a non-existent shoulder belt.

"Lap belt," Curt said.

She found it buried in the bench seat beside her and got it buckled and cinched up tight. She rescued the steel mug from between her clenched knees and took a sip, trying not to dump it down her shirt on the dirt road.

With his eyes still on the road ahead, Curt said, "Seriously, Neets, why you packing?"

"I always carry a gun."

"Not always, or you'd have shot my ass when I come around the corner and scared you."

"Well, I don't sleep with the damn thing! Can we just drop it?" She ignored the tense silence issuing from the other side of the truck, and stared out her window. The pines lining the road were a dusty green after a month without rain. Behind their ragged edge, she could see the clear cut acres stretching to the north and west.

Logging in East Texas was big business—and staying out of the way of the log trucks barreling down the small roads wasn't always easy. She had breathed a sigh of relief when they had finished logging the piece of land nearest hers.

When you've got tons of truck carrying even more tons of missile-shaped logs, it's a recipe for disaster. She could see from here the thousands of seedlings another crew had planted a few weeks after the cut.

He sighed. "Let's call off the hostilities, just for today, okay?"

"It's all right with me."

Curt flipped the radio on; the stiffened fingers of his right hand made it an awkward process. He tapped the fingers of his left on the steering wheel to the rhythm of the country song that played from the single, tinny speaker in the dash.

"So what really happened to your hand?" she asked over the music.

"I told you—I put it through a glass shower door."

"How?"

"I was reaching for a towel and I slipped."

"Really?"

"Nope, made it up."

"Really?

"Would you stop saying really?"

"Would you start telling me the truth?"

"Damn it!" His voice was a near shout. "You agreed we'd play nice for one day."

"I'm sorry. No, really," and she shot him a lopsided grin.

He frowned. "Now the old man's dead, I guess I can tell you. But you can't say anything to the family about it."

"The old man? You mean Tucker? He did that to you?" Flak's voice rose with each question.

"He didn't know it was me." Curt made the turn onto paved road.

Flak reached over and turned the radio off. "So talk."

"You know Mama died in July of '99."

"I remember. What's that got to do with it?"

"You're going to have to shut up if you want to hear this."

"Shutting up, sir." Flak saluted. She loosened her seatbelt, and turned so she could see his face, her back to the door, one foot folded under her. She studied him over her frequent sips of coffee as he spoke.

"Yeah, right. Anyway, we got through Mama's funeral and everything, and I knew the rest of the bunch weren't going to tell him she was gone. I went down where I knew Daddy parked his camper, near Sam Rayburn." He paused and Flak nodded.

"He was already half deaf by then, and he didn't hear me coming. I guess. I knocked on the door of the camper, and he came boiling out swinging a machete. Thing must have been two, two-and-a-half foot long.

When he swung it down on me, I just reached up to grab the blade and keep it off my face. He sliced me from here to here."

Curt drove with his knee long enough to run his left index finger down the scar running from the webbing between the middle and ring fingers on his right hand all the way to his wrist. He turned it over and she saw the matching white lines carved into his palm.

"It was razor sharp. Took two years of physical therapy to get it this good. I'm lucky I can still use my hand at all. End of story."

Flak sat stunned. "Oh my God. The girls told me he tried to kill you with a truck, not a machete."

"Oh he did that, too."

"Why the hell would you take that man in and take care of him?"

"I had a very good reason."

"Good grief, what?"

Curt pulled the truck into the store's lot, stopped, put it in gear and stepped on the emergency brake before he answered.

"Mama asked me to."

"But she was dead!"

"Oh, hell, before she died. She said nobody else would take care of him. She was right." He shrugged, and got out of the truck, but leaned back in the open window. "I meant what I said, Neets. Not a word to the family about it."

Flak nodded. After she got out of the truck, she took a moment to admire what had been done to the store already. The canopy had been restored, as had the roof.

As they walked toward the front of the store, she noted the outer door was now on straight, with new screening. He put one hand on it before she could get it open.

"Not a word, Flak. They don't need anything else to hate him for. Promise?"

"Promise."

Curt banged on the inner door with his good hand. "Hey, Mags, it's me!"

Maggie opened it almost immediately. "Hey, I was afraid you weren't going to come out."

Flak stepped into her view.

"Ah. Anita, how are you?"

"Fair to middlin'."

"Yes. Well." Maggie took a deep breath, but Flak anticipated her.

"I'm just here to help paint, Maggie. And maybe to ask Frederick a few questions. Is he here?"

"No. He said he'd come by later." She made shooing motions to move them back away from the door.

Maggie winced as the shriek went up once more from the tortured metal when she pulled it shut, and stood, both hands toying with the doorknob behind her.

"I have to get it oiled." She paused a moment. "Anita, Jenny's having a really good day today— and I want to keep it that way." She stared into Flak's eyes.

Flak nodded. "I understand."

"Do you?"

"I think so, Maggie. I'll keep it light around her."

Maggie's shoulders relaxed. She turned the knob behind her and backed into the doorway, nearly toppling Jenny, who stood behind it with a paint can in each hand.

"I thought I heard the door! Hey, big brother. Anita." She nodded briskly at Flak.

"Where do you want to start, Curtis Lee?"

He eyed the two gallons she held up for his inspection. "I hope you got more than that."

"You betcha, red rider. We have gallons and gallons out back. Mags went crazy at Sherwin Williams."

She must have noted Flak's flinch at the word "crazy."

"That's the good part about being a nut job, darlin'. I get to say what I want, when I want. A little ironic I live in Looneyville now, don't you think?"

Flak's "um" was lost in what sounded like forced laughter from Maggie and Curt.

"The key," Jenny continued, "is to make sure your manic-depressives are in manic phase when it's time to start painting. We get so much more done."

She spun and headed for the back of the store. "Get your tools off the truck and let's get going."

Curt gave a Maggie a quick, one-armed hug. "I see she's on the road to recovery. How're you doing?"

"Better." Flak saw an unspoken message pass between them, but wasn't sure what it was.

"Curtis Lee!" came a shout from the back.

"Coming! Keep your shirt on."

The morning passed quicker than Flak could have imagined. She'd gotten used to the smell of paint when she'd been married to Curtis, but it wasn't in her top ten favorites. The solidity of the scent got up her nose, made her feel cut off somehow. She never realized how much she depended on her sense of smell until something took it away.

Curt and Jenny kept up their rapid-fire banter while they painted the outside of the store. Flak stayed in earshot, but out of the conversation.

"Do you remember when Tucker brought the pigs home?" Jenny had been in the "do you remembers," for the latter part of the morning, but their father's name had been absent until now.

"Hoo, Mama was mad, wasn't she?" Curt laughed. "Especially when he named them after Grandma and Aunt Sue and Aunt Robbie."

"Not near as mad as him bringing them home without building a pen first." Jenny's smile sounded in her voice.

The brother and sister were around the corner from her, but Flak couldn't help smiling in response. If Curt had been half as tender with her as he was with his sister, she reflected, their marriage might have stood half a chance.

"Man, I worked my ass off building that pen. You know how Daddy was about everything being perfectly straight and absolutely level, even for a pigpen."

"Well, I worked my ass off scrubbing the living room from top to bottom after we moved 'em to the pen. Mama swore she could still smell pig, even after we'd scrubbed blisters onto our hands.

I smelled like a swimming pool for weeks from all the chlorine bleach. Not that we knew what a pool smelled like." Jenny paused, and Flak heard the pair say together, "Because we were too poor to have a pool!"

"You ever get in an 'I grew up poorer than you' contest with your friends?"

The sounds of paintbrushes slapping on bare walls hid Curt's response.

"I always won them at the booby hatch. I'm not sure most poor people can afford to go crazy."

Flak wondered how crazy Jenny actually was. Crazy enough to steal a jar of rocket fuel from God only knows where and then set it up to send Tucker to a fiery death?

Didn't seem like a woman's crime, somehow, but she'd heard weirder things. Like the gal a few years back ran over her husband three times with her truck after he messed around on her.

Her thought process was interrupted by a horn sounding out front.

Jenny said, "It's Ben!"

Flak rounded the corner and spied Curt up on a ladder, painting left-handed.

"I thought you were right-handed," she said without thinking.

"Nothing like getting your hand cut off to make you ambidextrous."

"Sorry."

He smiled down at her. "It's okay. I'm used to it."

He finished the patch he was working on, and stepped down the ladder. "It's time to break anyway. Nearly noon."

Curt pulled a roll of plastic wrap out of a box, tore off a strip and handed it to Flak. She looked at it like it was a snake.

"Wrap it around the brush. It'll keep it from drying out while we're taking a break. Didn't I teach you anything while we were together?"

"Not about painting." She wrapped the brush as ordered, and laid it on top of a paint can he'd re-lidded.

Ben and Jenny had already walked in the store. The doors were open front and back, and the lights off. Flak sighed when she hit the cooler air inside. She hadn't realized how hot she was until then.

Maggie walked up with a huge glass of iced tea for her and a Dr Pepper for Curt. "Hope you like it unsweet—I can break open some sugar if you need it."

"Not for me," Flak said, and drank half the glass. She wiped her mouth and saw Curt looking at her.

"What?"

"Nothing."

Ben and Jenny came from the back dragging folding chairs and set them up. Curt and Flak sank in them with identical sighs.

"You got anything stronger than Dr Pepper?" Ben asked Maggie.

"No, sorry."

He shrugged. "No biggie," and leaned against the open door frame.

"There's another chair in the house, if you feel like getting it," Maggie said.

"That's okay—I've been driving all week, and got more to do. Standing feels good."

"Aren't you staying to help paint?" Jenny asked.

He shook his head. "Can't. Got a gig down in College Station, have to get down there and help the boys set up." He brought the foot down from the door frame, and started tapping the toe of his boot, as if he were hearing the music in his head.

"We were just talking about the time when Tucker brought those pigs home, and we had to build a pen for them. You remember that?" Jenny was still in memory mood, obviously.

Ben said, "That's kind of rude, don't you think?"

Jenny looked the question at him.

"With the Sheriff of Nacogdoches County here and all, you ought not to be talking about pigs—she could take it all wrong." The sly note in Ben's voice grated on Flak.

"Don't bother me," she said, and took another long drink of her tea. "But I can see you might resent the reference, being an asshole and all."

Maggie, Curt and Jenny burst out laughing, and Ben took a deep breath. "Well now I see why you divorced her, little brother. That mouth is sharp."

"Weeelll," Curt drawled, "A, we ain't divorced. And B, I wouldn't piss my wife off too bad if I was you—her mouth ain't the only weapon she's packing."

Maggie and Jenny looked at Ben, as if to see if he'd return the verbal serve. His response wasn't long coming.

"So you need a bodyguard now?" Flak kept silent with an effort. She'd already stirred the pot enough with her first ill-considered remark.

Curt's voice was calm, but his eyes were not. "No, but you might want to watch your back—you never know who might be walking up behind you."

"What you going to do, set me on fire?"

"That's enough!" Maggie's firm statement was enough to stop the pair in their tracks. Flak realized she didn't just look like Miz Emlyn, she sounded like her, too.

"If you two can't act like adults, then I don't want you here."

Ben straightened from the doorjamb. "Well, I guess that's my cue. I'll just head on down to Aggieland, and leave y'all to it. Don't talk about me too much while I'm gone."

He tipped the cowboy hat to his sisters. "Ladies." He strode off to the beat-up Caddy. The four of them remained silent until he peeled out of the lot, throwing gravel on Curt's pickup like a cat finishing its business in a litter box.

"That last remark," Maggie said to Flak, "in case you didn't know it, was a reference to our family sport."

Flak looked at her, waiting for an explanation.

"We have a tendency to talk about whoever leaves—we all know it, we all do it. It's a standard family goodbye."

Flak shook her head. "I don't know about y'all sometimes."

Jenny laughed. "I got news for you—at least I know I'm crazy. Got a piece of paper and everything. The rest of this bunch think they're sane."

"You are not crazy," Maggie said between her teeth. "You just had a little trouble coping, that's all."

"Am, too," Jenny said, but her voice was gentle. "I am too crazy."

CHAPTER TWELVE
Jenny

I know you think I'm crazy now—but you should have seen me in those last few months after my sister left.

The last time he tried to hurt me was right after the blowup with her. Her bravery did something inside my head. Just the fact she'd stood up in front of him and said what she thought and she wasn't dead. I was fourteen, going on fifteen, and I told him I would slit his wrinkly old throat.

Seriously. I'd lean over the table and put my fists on it, and tell him right in his face.

"I'm crazier than you are, old man."

That's when I knew it was almost over. He didn't even threaten to hit me.

Mama had her first heart attack the day after we up and left him. I got to erase what he'd done to me and just start over, but I couldn't fix Mama's heart.

I guess, to a certain extent anyway, she fixed it herself. She lived for twenty-two more years after her first attack. She'd spent twenty-one years in her marriage, so it seems like it was almost adequate payback. Now.

Mama and my sister and I, we bore the brunt of it. He haunted all of us, I guess, but it was harder on us than on the boys. Not that you'd get them to admit that. They all got to escape in their own ways. We were stuck. Do you know we had a baby sitter even when my oldest sister was seventeen? The old man just knew we'd set the house on fire by actually turning on the stove or something if we were there by ourselves.

For my sister and me, we had decades of nightmares. I tried to drown all the hurts and the memories in booze and drugs. She did it with geography, traveling all over the world with the military.

I gave the booze and the drugs and the pain up to God, and lost her in the process. She couldn't see I was still there under the trappings of faith. When I lost touch with God after Mama's death, though, she was right there. She's been there ever since. Now I have both God and my sister, and I like it that way.

The boys think she wants to be Mama—wants to take on this huge gaping hole where our mother used to be in our family.

I know better. She is Mama.

Oh, stop looking at me like that. I'm not falling off the nut tree again. I could have probably put it better, though.

She's what Mama might have been in a different time and place. Strong, caring, smart, verbal, creative. She does look like Mama some, but it's more about an expression and a tone of voice than anything.

My sister is what Mama should have been.

CHAPTER THIRTEEN

By four o'clock, the outside of the small building had taken on the pristine look fresh paint gives the most battered outlook. Jenny painted for hours in silence, with infrequent pauses, apparently listening to something only she could hear. Flak and Curt traded enough words to work efficiently, no more.

Curt swabbed one last time at the eave he was painting, and said, "That's it," to the two women standing at ground level. "Let's get this stuff cleaned up."

Jenny pointed at the bucket of water next to her. Curt said, "Oh, you're waiting on me?" She nodded. He took a step down the ladder and paused. "Hey, there's Frederick." He finished his descent and dropped his brush in the bucket of water Jenny had readied.

A red, late-model Cadillac, gleaming with wax, pulled in the lot with two people in it. Flak turned to look at the car and said sideways to Curt, "You the only brother doesn't drive a Caddy?"

"Yep," he said, and squatted to rinse the paint from the brush.

He hoisted the bucket and brush and moved to the pasture next to the store to dump the water. Flak realized Jenny was nowhere to be seen. "Where'd your little sister go?"

Curt shrugged. He took the damp rag Flak had slung over her shoulder and began wiping his hands and the handle of the brush down.

A sandy-haired man got out of the vehicle on the driver's side, one of the few people Flak had ever seen where the term barrel-chested was accurate—he was as big around as a fifty-five-gallon drum. None of it seemed to be fat, either.

He went around the front of the car and opened the woman's door. She was dressed as if for church, dishwater blonde hair pulled back in a neat ponytail at the nape of her neck. She was the same height as her husband, and not exactly tiny herself. Flak tried to remember her name. Arlene? Lurleen? Something like that.

"Maggie's inside—we'll be right there!" Curt yelled at his brother.

"What's his wife's name?" Flak whispered.

"Don't you remember?"

"I only met her a couple of times, and it was years ago. She didn't make much of an impression."

Curt's mouth twisted as if from a bad taste, and he began putting the tools of his trade together. "You were lucky—Raylene must have been on her best behavior."

"Raylene—yeah, that was it. Didn't you tell me she got the horse's butt of the year award one Christmas?"

"Yep," Curt matched her quiet tones. "She made Maggie cry that year. She was one of the reasons Mama started that particular tradition."

"Maggie? I thought she was tough as nails."

"She is when she's got somebody to defend. Her self-defense skills are a little on the short side."

"What happened?"

"You'd have to ask Mags for the details."

"Damn it, I wish y'all would stop that."

"What?"

"Every time I get close to any information, one of you says, 'Well you'll have to ask them about it.' It's like playing human pinball."

Curt laughed. "I'm sorry. Really, I don't know the details. I found Maggie at Mama's house crying on Christmas Day. She babbled something about Raylene telling her the Mormon Tabernacle Choir was singing from the pits of hell. That's all I know." He drew an X on his chest. "Cross my heart."

"Fine. I was just curious."

"Just female, more like," Curt said, and grabbed the ladder to haul it to the truck.

"I am occasionally, you know."

"Believe me, I know. Grab the bucket of brushes, would you?"

Flak finished helping him load the truck, and stole a glance in his side mirror while she was at it. She knew she looked awful, but there wasn't much she could do about it. She smoothed the red curls as best she could, but the heat and humidity bounced them right back.

Curt said, "You look fine, come on. Here's your chance to pistol-whip Frederick." He leaned close to her ear as she walked beside him. "Think you could take Raylene out while you're at it?" She lobbed him a dirty look, and stepped back to let him go first through the door and into the store.

"Hello, Frederick," Curt said as he entered. Flak blinked a few times to adjust her eyes to the dimness.

"Hey, bud."

Curt introduced her. "Frederick, Raylene, you remember Anita." Both nodded.

Maggie came bustling past the now fully stocked shelves and handed an iced tea and Dr Pepper over to Flak and Curtis Lee. The smell of Raylene's perfume overwhelmed the smell of fresh paint and Windex. It was like being strangled by flowers.

"You sure I can't get you two anything?" Maggie asked Frederick and his wife. "I'll be happy to bring you some tea or coffee."

"No, thank you," Raylene said. "We're fine. We can't stay."

"There's a lot of that going around." Maggie smiled. "Ben stopped in for just a minute, but he split in a big hurry."

"Well, Freddie got a call a little while ago asking him to come back in early." Raylene's shrill tones were like listening to a buzz saw cut through sheet metal. Flak struggled to keep her face deadpan, when what she wanted was to grimace and cover her ears. The torture continued.

"He's only been home a week, but they just can't seem to do without him anymore."

"Ben still singing?" Frederick asked Maggie.

"Said he had a gig down in College Station."

"Where's Jenny?"

"In the house, I imagine."

Flak couldn't quite identify the split-second emotion that flashed across his face. She wished she knew what was going through his head. He pulled one of the folding chairs up and sat facing Flak and Curt, who had collapsed into their own already.

Raylene moved behind Frederick and laid a hand on each of his shoulders. The faceted stones making up the numerous rings on her hands caught every available spark of light. The impeccably manicured hands had plenty of space. When Frederick crossed his arms, the shoulders seemed to expand even more. Flak wondered if he'd even needed shoulder pads in his high school football days.

She cleared her throat. Feeling the glare Curt shot at her sideways, she plowed forward anyway.

"This is just a formality, Frederick, but I need to know where you were on the fifteenth of this month."

"Why?" Raylene asked.

Flak said in level tones. "Like I said, it's just a formality. I've asked everyone in the family for the same information." Maggie and Curt both nodded.

The man's voice was nowhere near as big as he was, it was downright mild. Maybe he was trying to make up for Raylene's tones.

"I was up near Wichita Falls. We've got forty-two wells up there I had to inspect."

"Can you prove it?" Flak saw Raylene stiffen, and hoped the woman would keep her mouth shut. From what little she remembered of her, it was probably a vain hope.

The big man nodded, and the pleasant expression on his face changed not one whit. "Sure—I'll get you a copy of the motel receipts. I was up there for about a week."

"And he called me every night. I'll show you the phone bill if you don't believe it." Raylene bit off each word and spat them at Flak. "This is about that evil old man, isn't it?"

Flak nodded. "Yes, it's about Tucker's death."

"He was satanic, demon-possessed." Raylene shook herself, like a dog just stepping out of a rain shower. "There was no justice on this earth sufficient for that demon in human skin. There is no city of refuge for those who face God's judgment—and he will burn for all eternity." Her voice got louder with every word.

Flak discarded a few possible answers and said, with as little confrontation in her voice as she could muster, "I don't doubt that in the slightest. I'm just trying to find out if someone here on Earth helped him get to that meeting a mite early."

"It's all right, honey," Frederick said, patting the hand still gripping his shoulder. "It's okay, really. Anita's just doing her job."

He continued, "And I see you're doing a fine job here as well."

"Pardon?" Flak was completely in sheriff mode, had no idea what he was talking about.

He waved his hand to indicate their surroundings. "The store—the paint job looks great."

"Oh! That was mostly Curt's doing."

"You and Jenny helped a lot, and Mags did all the work in here." Curt interrupted. "But look, folks—we got to get back to town. I need to clean up, and Anita... well, Anita has to clean house. It's a wreck."

They said their goodbyes and Curt dragged Flak out to the truck by the elbow. She wrenched it away from him long enough to get in, and rounded on him when got behind the wheel.

"What the heck was that all about?"

"You got what you needed." Curt put the truck in gear, and pulled out of the parking lot headed toward Flak's house.

"Well, did you have to trash my housekeeping while you were at it?"

"Sorry. It was the best I could come up with on short notice."

"The best what?"

"Excuse to get the hell away from her. It's like listening to fingernails on a chalkboard—she makes my brain want to explode."

Flak remained silent. She couldn't argue with his assessment. Raylene was never going to win any Miss Congeniality awards.

Curt downshifted around a curve. "Plus, you were busy with Frederick, and didn't see the way she was looking at you. I did. She's pathologically jealous of any woman who even looks at Frederick, much less talks to him. If looks could kill, you'd have a hole right between your eyes."

"Pathologically, huh?"

"Yeah, it's my new word for the week." Curt glanced over at Flak. "Oh, no, I'm not trying to add Raylene to your list of suspects here."

"How come she hates Tucker as much as the rest of you?"

Curt threw his hands in the air, but slapped them back down on the wheel immediately as the truck began to drift left. "You'd have to ask her."

He pushed the old trucks gearshift down into fourth. "But, if I had to guess, I'd say there's a fair chance he made a pass at her at some point. That's why I never took you around him—I didn't want to have to kill him."

Flak just looked at him.

"Damn it, Anita, stop taking everything I say literally."

"Okay, fine. You know your family so much better than I do—you tell me which one killed him. You say you didn't. Then who did?"

"Ben." He grinned at her.

"Ben's the only one of the bunch with a legitimate alibi."

"Frederick just told you he has motel receipts."

"From a week-long stay in a motel that's about five-six hours drive away. Motels don't check on their occupants. He could have driven down here at any time."

"How about the phone calls?"

Flak smiled. "Bet you dollars to donuts he has a cell phone. Doesn't matter where he calls from." She thought for a few seconds, "Although, I'll bet the bills would tell us which cell tower he was near. If I can get a warrant for them, which won't be easy."

"Dang."

"Yeah. If you hadn't dragged me out of there, I was going to ask him if he was using his cell or the phone at the motel."

Another thought occurred to her, and she started counting off on her fingers.

"Let's see. You say you were with a woman, but you won't name her. Maggie says she and Jenny were together, but Jenny probably won't remember, she's too spaced out. Which blows both of their alibis. Frederick's won't hold water. Where does that leave me?"

"With something that didn't even happen! I'm telling you, Neets, the old man was smoking in bed."

"The evidence says otherwise."

"What evidence?" He shouted the words, surprising her.

"I'm sorry—I'm already talking to you too much about it. You're too close to all of this, to all of them."

"I did not kill him. No one in my family killed him." A vein throbbed on the side of Curt's head, below the edge of the paint-splattered baseball cap he wore. "We've gone over all this."

"Actually, I believe you didn't kill him."

"Then why won't you telling me what's going on?"

She shook her head. "You're too close to your family."

He threw his hands up in the air. "Then you think one of them did it."

"I didn't say that."

"Grrrf." He growled.

He reached past her knee, flipped open the glove box, yanked out a pack of Marlboros and a lighter, and lit one.

"You know, that's the first cigarette I've seen you light today."

"I was trying to quit," he said, and blew out a lungful of smoke. "Guess it ain't happening today."

The rest of the trip was silent. The trees arched over the little farm-to-market road, as the rackety old truck sped through green, leafy tunnels and swooping curves. Wildflowers drooped in the heat, but still lent riotous color to the sunny areas of the roadside.

Curt lit one cigarette straight from the other. Flak chose to make no comment. By her count, it was his fifth one he was rubbing out in the filthy ashtray as they pulled into her drive.

Sitting on the hood of his car, legs stretched out in front of him and his back to the road, was Garvey.

"What the hell is he doing here?" Curt growled at her.

"What's that got to do with you?"

"Nothing. Not one, single, solitary thing."

Flak hopped out of the truck. "Hey, Garv, what's up?"

The big man turned and stood. "Hey, girl. Not much. Just a little worried about you. Saw the cruiser and stopped, but you didn't answer the door. Was just deciding whether to check inside or not."

"She was safe with me," Curt said, leaning against his truck, arms folded.

"I reckon she probably was." Garvey's tone and demeanor remained relaxed.

The silence afterward seemed awkward to Flak.

"Ahem. Well—I guess I better feed Andy and see if Barney's showed up."

Garvey stopped her with a hand on her arm. In her peripheral vision, she could see Curt's good hand clench into a fist.

"What's up with Barney?"

She looked up at him. "I haven't seen him since last night. He never came back."

"You want me to look for him?"

"I already checked the woods this morning, he wasn't there." Curt said.

"Oh, really?"

"Yeah, really."

Falk yanked her arm out of Garvey's grasp. "Look—if you two want to slug it out over who's going to go look for the dog, that's fine. I'm going to go feed my cat."

She strode off toward the back of the house. She never went in the front door; wasn't even sure where the key was.

The air conditioning felt like a spring shower after the lack of any cooling in Curtis's truck. Andy was sprawled on her bed, on his back, flat as a pancake.

She sat beside him and began rubbing his furry tummy, lost in thought. A few moments later, she jerked her hand just away in time to keep it unbitten. "Hey!"

The cat didn't even have the grace to look apologetic, just rolled away from her and licked his fur where she'd disarranged it.

The air conditioning caught up to the thermostat setting and the fan stopped. She realized she could hear Curt and Garvey still talking outside.

She carefully slid enough of the bedroom window blind down so she could see without being seen, and saw Curt throw his head back, laughing. The two turned to walk toward the back of the house, and Curt, still smiling, slapped Garvey on the back.

Flak moved to the back door and watched the pair split up as they headed toward the tree line.

She shook her head, turned to go to the bathroom and tripped over Andy. He looked up at her and purred, one burst of kitty rumble. "You're just like 'em," she told him, and headed for the shower.

CHAPTER FOURTEEN
Jenny

I hated dolls, wouldn't play with them. They weren't interesting—in fact, they were kind of creepy. My sister was none too fond of them, either, although she did at least give them names. Or actually, a name. She named them all Cindy. And then ignored them right along with me.

Our father decided we weren't interested in dolls because they weren't realistic enough. You have to understand, he didn't actually ask us what we thought. So he cut the hair off a couple of generic ones to make boy dolls. It didn't work. We still weren't interested.

Mama never gave up, though, so we had this long shelf in our room filled with dusty, lonely dolls. Sis and I played with stuffed animals. We weren't even slightly creative with their naming— there was Orange Dog, Brown Dog and Gray Kitty, just to name a few of them. And the Pelican. But he was wooden and his jaw opened up and his wings whirled when you rolled him across the floor. I kept all of them for years after I grew up—left them behind in a move.

One year, Mama made us gigantic stuffed whales, as big as we were, out of these bright-colored, terry-cloth towels she got for free in boxes of detergent. The next year, it was snakes, made from the same thing. We loved them.

Why animals instead of dolls? I don't know. Maybe because they were safe. As far as we knew, animals never hurt you. The only nature show we ever saw was Wild Kingdom, and as long as you were Marlon Perkins, you were okay. He was perfectly willing to risk life and limb, as long as it was his helper, Jim's life and limbs on the line.

I guess I'm rambling today—sorry. But then, one of the things I've learned since I've been going over all this in my head is that, as bad as growing up was, it wasn't bad every minute of every day.

It just seems like that in my memory.

CHAPTER FIFTEEN

Flak woke reaching for Barney's ears to give them a scratch. Patting the empty spot where the dog should be, she remembered the men hadn't found him the night before. Curt stuck his head in the back door after their search, and asked if she wanted to join him and Garvey at the Sports Shack for a beer. She had declined, with thanks.

She sighed and got out of the bed. The coffee filter put up the usual struggle, but she finally got the wake-up brew going.

She was still freezing from waking without the big mutt's friendly warmth, and headed for the thermostat to turn the air conditioning down. To speed the warming, she unfastened the back door and pushed the screen door to prop it open. After six inches, it stopped dead. She pushed harder, and it moved enough to let her squeeze outside.

The hairy form was too familiar to mistake. The door slipped from her nerveless fingers and closed with a bang.

"Oh, Jesus." Flak went to her knees beside the body of the dog. His fur was matted with dirt and damp from the morning dew. No sign of breath stirred his ribcage. She pulled the long hair away from his ugly, beloved face, and found the hole just behind his eyes. Reaching under his head, she was sure what she'd find, but no exit hole met her fingers. Her tears dripped on his muddy fur as she gathered him into her arms.

She grunted with the effort to stand and walked around the house with her burden. She opened the back door of the cruiser with one hand, nearly losing her balance, and placed him carefully in the back seat.

Flak ran back around the house, scrambled into enough clothes to be decent and headed toward town. Halfway in, she came out of her fog long enough to check with dispatch.

"Dorrie—get Doc Adams on the phone and tell him I'll meet him at the morgue."

"Any problem?"

"No, nothing worth talking about. Just have him meet me there." The effort to control her voice took everything she had.

"Yes, ma'am."

Flak turned off the lights and siren she'd flipped on automatically and brought her speed back to the limit. It would take a while to roust the doc out, and it was far too late for Barney.

Doc Adams came in the door of the morgue grousing. "Some people don't know its Sunday. Dang heathens."

At the sight of the hairy form lying on the single stainless steel table, he stopped. "Oh, come on, Flak, I'm a people cutter, not a doggie doctor."

She took a deep breath, inhaling the smells of formaldehyde and disinfectant. "I need what's in his head, Doc. It's evidence."

"Evidence of what? Some near-sighted hunter thought the dog was a deer?"

She shook her head. "It doesn't matter. Just get me a bullet, if there's enough left of it to get, and an approximate time of death."

"It'll be really approximate."

"I don't care. Do what you can."

Flak stuck it out as long as she could, long enough for the coroner to tell her the powder burns around the wound meant the shot had been from point blank range. When the doctor pulled out the bone saw, she gave up. She'd attended more than one autopsy during her training, but never for a friend.

She walked around the building three times, pushing down the grief and anger with each step. She kept thinking of the way Barney had looked when she'd found him at the pound.

It had been right after she got the house, and he was in that clumsy teenager stage that puppies get to right before they get their full growth, all paws and hair. When she stopped by the cage he sat in all alone, he had looked her in the eye, and gave only one wag of his beautiful tail—it seemed he had given up on anyone taking him home. The animal shelter attendant told her he was due to be euthanized the next day—he'd been there two weeks. She'd picked Andy up the same day.

As she neared the outer door of the tiny building on her fifth lap, the doctor came out of the building drying his hands on a paper towel. He reached in his pocket and handed her a clear evidence bag.

"Near as I can tell, even though it's pretty smashed up, that's a .22. That's why there was no exit wound." His voice deepened into lecture mode.

"You know, they call the .22 an assassin's bullet. It's got enough punch to enter a human's body, but not enough to exit, so it ricochets inside, causing more damage. It went through his skull at an angle and then bounced around in there quite a bit."

Flak took the bag from him and held it where she could see it, staring down at death in metal form. The anger continued to build.

Doc Adams laid one hand on her shoulder.

"Was he yours?"

She nodded.

"Well, if it helps any, he didn't suffer. He was dead pretty much instantly." The doc dropped his hand.

Shaking her head, "It doesn't help."

"I'm sorry."

Flak was unable to tell him it was okay. "How long was he dead?"

"Hard to tell—did some math with temperatures and such, tried to divide it out by his body weight, but the best I can do is give you a range."

"And?"

He sighed. "My best guess—somewhere between twenty-four and forty-eight hours."

"He was alive thirty-six hours ago."

"Then it was after that, but not too long after." Doc Adams paused a moment. "Where did you find him?"

"On my back steps when I got up this morning."

"No way he got there on his own—somebody had to have put him there."

Flak motioned for him to continue.

"He was covered with dirt—every inch of him, even in the wound. Somebody buried him, and then thought better of it."

Flak remained silent, her mind spinning through the possibilities. The only major case on her plate was Tucker Barnes' death. Who was warning her off?

The doc interrupted her thoughts, "I'll have Jerry pick him up and take him out to the pet crematory."

"No."

He sighed, and shook his head. "Then let me get him in a bag for you. Give me a minute."

"Yeah. Thanks."

Outside, she leaned back on the hood of her cruiser, deep in thought. One more set of alibis to check—the bullet was in bad shape, but maybe they could get enough to confirm or reject her hypothesis. And it was a whole lot easier than thinking about what was coming out of the door.

Ten minutes later, Doc Adams came out with the shapeless, heavy bag, and she opened the trunk for him. She couldn't slam the cover, she just leaned her weight on the trunk lid, heard it secure with a click.

Flak couldn't look the doc in the eye—afraid the pity on his face would undo her.

Staring down at her boots, she said, "Look, Doc, I need one more favor."

"Name it."

"Don't say anything to anyone about this."

"I have to put the paperwork together on it, or it won't stand up in court."

She nodded. "I know. Just… file it in your desk drawer for now, okay?"

"You're the sheriff." The doctor shrugged. "But be careful."

She moved around the side of the car and opened the door. He came after her, put his hand on her shoulder again before she could get in.

"I mean it, Flak. Somebody's trying to tell you something with this."

"Well, I just developed a hearing problem."

He dropped his hand with a sigh, and she slid behind the wheel.

Flak drove through the Sunday morning church traffic, ignoring the telltale brake lights of speeders who slowed at sight of the cruiser.

On arrival at the little house, she headed inside for the phone.

"Hey, Dorrie. No, everything's all right. Just didn't want to put out on the radio I'd picked up a raccoon some hunter shot up."

At Dorrie's question, "No, he didn't make it. I'm just going to bury him out back."

She hung up the phone with a sigh for the lies, and headed for the shed to get a shovel. She knew the quicker she could get Barney in the ground, the better, particularly in the July heat.

Propping the shovel against a tree, she made a quick reconnaissance into the woods, walking along the edge where she was just out of sight of the house.

She found a shallow hole near the northwest corner of her property, pine needles and leaf litter mounded around it as if something had been removed from it hastily, with no attempt to cover it back up or smooth it over.

Moving around the site in ever-widening circles, she found nothing.

"Only in the movies," she muttered to herself, "Does the killer conveniently drop a book of matches."

From long experience, she knew the pine needles would not show tracks, but hoped to find something, anything.

Eventually, she made her way back to the makeshift grave and squatted beside it. Once she hunkered down, she found she could see the house very clearly through the gap between the undergrowth and the lowest branches of the towering pines.

Flak grabbed the shovel on the way to the other side of her property, as far from the grave Barney's killer had dug as she could get. Clearing a space in the leaf litter and pine straw, she began to dig.

An hour later, she sat on the back porch, dirty, sweaty and exhausted after wrestling Barney's remains into the hole she'd dug. She'd been too busy to deal with the emotions, and welcomed the spark of anger that was all she had left.

When a woman walked around the corner of the house, she was too numb to be surprised.

"Hello, Maggie. I didn't hear a car. What can I do for you?" The question in her voice was negated by the flat delivery.

"I've been sitting out front for a while. Tried the front door bell, finally, but you didn't answer. I came to…" Maggie must have finally noticed that Flak's hands were filthy and she'd been sweating.

"Were you gardening? If I interrupted you, I'm sorry. I know it's your day off."

"No rest for the wicked."

She took in Maggie's appearance; fists buried in jeans pockets, and as soon as Flak looked her in the eye, she dropped her gaze, staring at the ground.

She traced figure eights on the ground with the toe of the tennis shoes she wore. Flak mustered up a weak chuckle.

"It's just something Dorrie tells me all the time."

Maggie watched her foot moving as if her life depended on it.

"Stay right there," Flak ordered. She went inside, washed her filthy hands and poured two glasses of iced tea.

She allowed the screen door to close with a bang behind her, and Maggie's head came up. Flak gestured with her head toward the table under the trees and led the way.

She sat down, tried not to think about what she had buried a few yards away, and sipped her tea in silence.

Maggie reached for the already-sweating glass Flak brought for her, and made a face at the bitter taste.

"Sorry, you drink sweet tea, don't you. I don't even keep sugar in the house."

"That's okay."

Flak pulled another chair around to put her feet up and slumped with a sigh. The silence lengthened, but she was feeling too ornery to make the first move.

Maggie finally broke the silence. "I wanted to talk to you about Jenny."

Flak didn't even open her eyes. "So talk."

"She's so fragile right now, Anita. I have to ask you not to come out again. She can't handle it." Maggie sat on the edge of her chair, feet crossed primly at her ankles.

"She can't handle it? Or you can't handle her?" Flak's inflammatory questions gave the lie to the mild tone in which she asked them.

"I do fine with her." Maggie paused. "But it's easier when she's not up in the air about something."

Flak took another sip of her tea. "I got a question for you. Does Jenny know how to shoot a gun?"

"What's that got to do with anything?"

"Just answer it."

Maggie shrugged. "All of us know how to shoot. Mama was a crack shot, and she taught me and Jenny. Tucker taught the boys how to handle a gun from the time they could walk."

Maggie looked puzzled.

Flak kept the questions going. "Do you own a gun?"

The small woman nodded. "A pistol. It was Mama's. Jenny doesn't even know where I keep it."

"But you do, don't you."

"Of course. What kind of question is that?" Maggie was starting to get mad; Flak could hear it in her voice.

"What kind of pistol?"

126

"A .22."

"Why don't you want Jenny to know where it is?" Flak tried to keep any hint of accusation out of her voice, but Maggie moved her feet under her, obviously poised to leave.

"I'm not stupid enough to give her access to a gun. She's tried to commit suicide twice."

"I only heard about once."

"I didn't tell the authorities about the second try."

"Why not?"

"Because it took me nearly a year to rescue her from the mental ward the first time."

Flak decided to push her a little bit. "Who designated you rescuer? What about your brothers?"

"Let's see." Maggie finally sat back in the chair. Her voice dripped with honeyed sarcasm.

"Ben's an alcoholic skirt-chaser. Frederick is not just holier than thou, he's holier than everybody. He would have taken her to church and prayed for her. Shrinks are like fairies and unicorns in his world—he doesn't believe in them."

Maggie bolted half the glass of tea, as if to try to drown the anger.

"What about Curt?"

Maggie paused, came to some decision. "Curtis Lee's the reason she tried the second time."

"Excuse me?"

"His letter tipped her over the edge."

"What letter?" Flak's mental ears perked up. New information, finally, from one of this tight-lipped family.

"The one he sent all of us demanding we give him money to support Tucker."

Flak shook her head.

"I'm sorry—I don't think I get it. Every one of y'all hated Tucker, and he wasn't even blood relation to Ben and Frederick. Why would Curt think you'd give him money?"

"Good question. You'd have to ask him."

"Damn it! Every one of you pulls the same crap on me."

Maggie shrugged again. "I have no idea why in the world he thought any of us would give him a dime. I just had to clean up the results."

"Why'd it blow Jenny off the branch, anyway?"

Maggie frowned. "She had actually been making good progress. She laughed occasionally, even joked around with my husband. She'd been wary of men for a long time, wouldn't be around most of them."

"So why'd she try to kill herself?"

Maggie shrugged. "It only made sense to her—I don't think it will help."

"Tell me anyway."

"She said no matter how hard she tried to keep Tucker out of her life, somebody kept dragging him back in. She took all the pills in order to erase him, finally and forever."

Flak sipped her tea, contemplating 'finally and forever.'

"What answer did you give Curt to his letter, anyway?"

"I told him to go pee up a rope."

It was the first time Flak had heard Maggie use

the language and accents of her childhood. Ordinarily, she spoke with the unaccented precision of a newscaster.

"And what was Curt's reaction to your answer?"

"Nothing, not a word."

"When did you and Jenny get your letters?" Flak lobbed the questions hard and fast, and hoped Maggie wouldn't simply get up and leave.

"March, I think. Might have been early April."

Flak kept pushing, trying to make all the pieces add up. "You said you called Frederick up for his birthday. When was that?"

"April 20."

"Ben and Frederick got the letter, too?"

Maggie nodded. "As far as I know."

"Why did it make you so mad? Other than Jenny's reaction, I mean."

"Extortion always makes me mad."

Flak smiled. "Calling it extortion's kind of rough, don't you think?"

Maggie snapped, "So is asking victims to send money to the criminal."

Flak shook her head. "I had one of my deputies check the records—Tucker was never charged with a crime."

Maggie shrugged once more. "Doesn't mean he didn't commit them. Just means he never got caught."

Flak spun the wheels of everything she'd learned in her mind, trying to make the cogs fit together. She realized there was one key piece only Maggie could give her.

"Look, Maggie. It's time to quit beating around the bush. Exactly what did Tucker do to you and Jenny?"

"I…" The confusion and pain on Maggie's face was evident, but she couldn't seem to get any words out.

"He's dead. He can't hurt you. Neither can the truth."

"I wouldn't bet on that," Maggie said.

"I would. What happened?" Flak pushed the impatience away. She knew it wouldn't help, and hoped it didn't show.

"It won't stand up in any court."

"I don't care. Tell me."

Maggie stood, as if sitting down had trapped her. She paced—first forward then she turned and took three steps the other way. She didn't look at Flak as she spoke.

"There are some things in this life that, when you talk about them, it pulls you back in, it makes you feel the same way you did at the time it happened."

She stopped talking, stopped walking, with her back to the sheriff. Flak maintained her silence.

"What Tucker did was…unforgivable. And now he's dead, he can't be punished like he should have been. So telling you does no good."

Maggie bowed her head, as if in prayer, for a few moments. Flak kept very still.

Never turning back toward her, she said, "Just stay away from Jenny, Anita. That's all you need to know."

Flak watched her walk toward the house and around it, and didn't try to stop her.

CHAPTER SIXTEEN

Jenny

I learned to sleep through the night without getting up to go to the bathroom because of him. No matter how much it hurts.

Comes in handy on long car trips.

The few times I couldn't make it all the way through the night, I'd ease the door open of the bedroom I shared with my sister, and walk as fast as I could to the bathroom.

No hallways, right, so I had to go through the kitchen. His door was on my right, and he always slept on the side of the bed nearest the kitchen. No matter how determined I was not to look that way, it was like a mouse trying not to look at a snake.

Just as I got in front of the door, he'd take a drag off of his cigar. He smoked them constantly. There he'd be, like some evil, naked Buddha figurine, lit by the glow of the hot end of that cigar.

It was like a preview of hell. I can still hear the crackle of a cigar being stoked into life. The reddish light it cast is the same light illuminating all my nightmares.

Even when he wasn't there, and I don't remember that, but there must have been some times he was gone, I was worried about it. You look around every corner long enough, it leaves you in a permanent state of terror.

You know, this is going to sound stupid, but I wrote him a letter after everything blew up. Years after, really. Told him how I felt about it all, in no uncertain terms. Very healthy, all kinds of closure, right? Until I got his answering letter. And made the mistake of reading it. He said, and I quote, "I don't regret anything I've ever done. I only wish I'd done more of it."

I went to my husband and told him we had to move. Right then. I was like thirty-two years old and there I was jumping at every shadow and peeking around every corner again. I moved my entire family, and made sure my father wouldn't know where we lived. After that, I could breathe again.

So, where does his answer to my closure letter leave me? He was glad he raped me. He as much as said it in writing. My father.

Half my genes come from that incredible moral vacuum. You see, he wasn't immoral by his own lights. In his view of the world, everything he did was okay. There just wasn't time to do as much of it as he wanted.

I was sitting in the stands at my husband's over-thirty basketball game once, with my kids and other kids climbing all over the bleachers. This little girl sits down beside me.

She pointed at this sweaty guy on the floor and says, "That's my daddy. Where's yours?" I didn't know what to say, so I said, "My daddy's dead." She started crying.

So did I.

CHAPTER SEVENTEEN

Flak looked up when her office darkened—nobody filled a doorway quite like Harley.

"Jerry said you wanted me?"

"Yeah—take this bullet and run it against the ones in the Barnes arson."

Harley reached out one beefy arm and snagged the evidence bag without stepping in the room.

"Where'd you get it?"

"Just log it in and run it," Flak snapped.

"Yes, ma'am. Anything else?"

"Prints."

"Sorry?" Harley's face showed the confusion her polite question tried to express.

"Prints from the butane tank. What'd we get?"

"Oh! Nothing usable—just Randy's where he tried to turn it off. Everything else was smudged. Not even a partial."

"Anything more on the background checks?"

"Nope. Kindjal Industries ain't talking about what Maggie Kovax did. They're citing national security—top secret stuff."

"Great. Just great."

Harley shrugged.

"Just run the bullet and let me know."

"Yes, ma'am!" Harley saluted and clicked her heels together. Flak ignored it and went back to the timeline she was putting together.

Matching the brothers and sisters against the calendar was a frustrating process. None of the times shut any of them out of the murder except Ben.

Flak sighed and started going back over the timing. It was like trying to put a two-hundred-piece jigsaw together with a hundred pieces missing.

The phone shrilled, catching her off guard. One hand to her chest, she answered it.

"Sheriff."

"Hey Flak, its Jim."

"Hey, man—you got anything for me?"

"Yeah, actually, I do."

"Well give it up, son. I really need a break on this one." Flak pushed enough papers aside to rest her elbows on the desk. Chin in hand, she listened.

"You remember the tip you gave me about Kindjal Industries?"

Flak nodded, "Yeah—I just talked to my deputy about that. They're stonewalling us."

"I called in a few favors and got some info out of them. They were working with the chemicals that left the traces we found for their new KEM, but of course, they wouldn't give me the details on what proportions."

Confused, she asked, "Chem as in chemical?"

"No. K-E-M. It stands for Kinetic Energy Missile. They're trying to get them ready for use in the Middle East. KEMS don't have warheads. They just use speed and mass to destroy incoming missiles or hardened structures, like bunkers."

"What does it mean to this fire?"

"The fuel has to be incredibly explosive to power these missiles," he explained patiently. "That's why a small amount did so much damage."

"How would one of my suspects get a small amount?"

"Might be easier than you think. They created a number of samples to farm the manufacture out."

"Come again?" As hard as she tried, her ignorance of the subject made her feel like she was trying to understand a foreign language.

"Kindjal gave samples out to a half-dozen companies to bid on refining the fuel."

"Was Garrison on the list?"

"That, I couldn't get for you. The guy I was talking to simply didn't know who was on the samples list. But it shouldn't be too hard to find out. Just call them. Once the fuel is out of research and development, the refiners who are bidding on it aren't a secret.

"Sounds like a grand idea. Thanks, man."

"No sweat—you need anything else, you just call me."

"I'll do that."

Flak sat back in her chair.

Harley stuck her head back in the door.

"It looks like the same gun, boss, most likely."

"Why 'most likely'?"

"The bullet you handed me was in bad shape—but what little rifling we could get off it matched exactly. Might hold up in court, might not."

"Thanks, Harl. Oh, and Harley," she said. The head reappeared.

"Didn't mean to get ratty on you."

"Just got a cup of coffee. You want one, boss? Might improve your temper…"

Harley grinned and ducked out of the doorway just before the wadded paper would have hit her between the eyes.

Flak could hear the big deputy chuckling as she headed back toward her desk.

Eight hours later, Andy wound around Flak's legs as she moved back and forth in the kitchen to gather ingredients for an omelet. She was too tired to deal with cooking a full dinner for one, and sick of frozen food.

"Good grief, cat," she said after she tripped over him the third time.

"What turned you into Mama's little butt wart all of a sudden?" She leaned down and scratched behind his ears. It brought a lump to her throat as she realized one more time she'd never be able to do the same with her dog.

"You're just lonely for Barney," she told the purring cat. Or maybe she told herself. She wasn't sure.

The kitchen filled up with the mouthwatering smells of onions and peppers fried in butter, and toasted bread. She finished putting it all together and sat down at the table. The first bite was halfway to her mouth when the doorbell rang. She looked at her plate with regret and headed for the front hall. Omelets just never tasted good cold, and didn't reheat for doodly.

The door stuck from long disuse, but she got it open after a few tugs and cuss words.

"What do you want?" she asked Curt through the screen door. He stood on the square of concrete that passed for a front porch with a straw Stetson in his hands, turning it over and over. Was he nervous?

"Okay, that was rude. But not unusual. I want to talk to you."

"About what?"

He looked over her shoulder at the part of the living room he could see. "Not here. Go for a ride with me."

"No." She started to shut the door on him.

"C'mon Neets."

She sighed. "Look, it's a work night. I been filling out papers all damned day. I'm tired, I'm hungry. I just want to eat my dinner and go to bed."

He crossed his heart, the old familiar gesture. "I won't keep you out long. I swear."

She glared at him. "You're just not going to give up, are you."

"Nope." He grinned.

"Fine."

She slammed the door and locked it, then realized how it probably looked. "I'll come around!" she yelled, and heard a faint "Okay," in return.

She stopped long enough to slip on her tennis shoes, checked to make sure Andy had food. She stopped herself before she checked the dog's food, and had to swallow hard.

She knew her grief and anger would lessen as soon as she figured out who had shot Barney—she really hoped it wasn't Curt.

As she levered herself into the truck seat, she reflected she'd seen more of the man in the last two weeks than she had over a number of the months they'd been married.

She remained mired in her memories long enough to lose track of where they were going, and said so.

"Down by the river." They were the first words Curt had spoken since she got in the truck. Maybe he'd been thinking the same things.

She realized she was letting one of the suspects in a murder case haul her off to a dark and lonely spot, and gave herself a quick mental kick in the pants. Even though she'd said she believed Curt didn't do it, what was she supposed to say? "Nope, you're still a suspect?"

She leaned away from the seat slightly and scratched her back under her t-shirt. While doing so, she checked to see if her belt holster was still there. It was. She'd worn it for so many years, she could no longer feel its presence, and putting it on was so automatic, she hadn't even remembered doing it.

Bringing her left knee up in the seat, she swiveled so she could see Curt's face.

"While I've got you here—or rather, you've got me here, I got a question for you."

"What's that?" He kept his eyes on the road, didn't look at her.

"Maggie told me about the letter."

"What letter?"

"The one you wrote your brothers and sisters asking for money to support Tucker."

Curt made the turn from the Loop onto South 59, and gassed the old truck. "Oh. That letter."

"Yeah—did you really expect to get the money?"

He lifted the shoulder nearest her in a half-shrug. "I was desperate. I'd just come off a long, hard winter with no work in sight. The old man's medicine cost the earth, and it wasn't covered by the government. Had to try something before we both starved to death."

"Did you get anything out of them?"

Curt snorted. "Mostly a hard time. Saint Frederick gave me a couple hundred dollars. Said it was out of the charity of his heart, the same charity he'd give a stranger. Ben and Maggie told me to go to hell. Jenny never said a word either way."

She took a deep breath, dragging in the familiar odor of cigarette smoke and paint that was part of Curt wherever he went. "How desperate were you?"

He shook his head. "Not desperate enough to kill him, if that's what you're driving at. His funeral put me right back in the hole."

"None of y'all happened to mention this when we were out there painting the store for Maggie."

Again, his right shoulder pulled up to his ear in the body's equivalent of "whatever," she found particularly annoying. "Ain't nothing to say. With Tucker dead, it all just faded away."

Flak felt the truck tires begin the rapid rat-a-tat sounding out the surface of the Angelina River Bridge. It had been repaired so much, it looked like an asphalt crossword puzzle, lines everywhere.

Just on the other side, Curt slowed and directed the truck through the grassy median, onto a much-used, much-rutted dirt path. Flak braced one foot on the truck floor and one hand on the dash to survive the passage.

Pausing at the northbound lanes, he gunned it to get up on and then across the highway. On the other side of the road, concrete picnic tables were illuminated by his headlights, and then became dark shapes in the moonlight.

Curt shifted to neutral and allowed them to roll down the inclined bank. In the headlights, Flak could see the river was well below the high water mark. The scorching July heat and lack of rain had diminished the Angelina to a muddy stream, colored terra cotta from the red clay it cut through.

Curt cut the engine near the last picnic table perched just above the high-water mark. He laid both arms along the top arc of the steering wheel, good hand gripping the damaged one at the wrist.

"Are we done talking about my family?"

Flak was puzzled. "Sure, I guess. For now, anyway."

"Good."

"What's up?" She watched him closely. She remembered the pose—it was the same place and same position he'd taken when he told her he was moving out. His fingers had interlaced then, as they couldn't now. She waited, content to let him speak.

"You remember I told you there was a woman with me the night Tucker died?"

She nodded. "Hard to forget—especially since she's your alibi, and you wouldn't give me her name."

"There was a good reason. Besides being a born gentleman, I mean." Curt turned his head long enough to grin at her, and quickly focused on his hands once more. "You know her."

"I do?" Flak wasn't surprised. She wasn't sure what she was feeling—but she was pretty sure she didn't want to hear what was coming next.

He nodded. "Yeah. It's Ellen Ransom. The mayor's wife. Soon to be ex-wife, actually."

"Ah." Flak wasn't sure what else to say, so she kept her response neutral. Her chest was starting to ache in the same old way.

The fact he'd been catting around with the mayor's wife made more sense of his refusal to share the name. Didn't stop the ache, though.

"She was afraid if anyone found out about us it would cause Bill a ration of grief. He's up for re-election in November."

She focused on the darkness outside the truck, and continued his thought for him.

"And if people knew his wife was out screwing around, it would hurt his chances."

"You know this town, Neets. These good old boys decide he can't take care of his wife's business, he won't stand a snowball's chance in hell."

"And this matters to you because…" Flak raised an eyebrow at him, though he was still staring at his hands. Was he afraid to face her?

"Because it matters to Ellen. She's got kids to raise. And she don't want to trash herself in front of the whole town, either. This town can be rough on women."

"Yeah, I know."

"I imagine you do. I was real proud of you getting elected. But you and I both know if you were girly and lacy, you wouldn't have made it. They want certain things in a sheriff, and certain things in a mayor's wife."

"No argument here." Flak knitted her fingers together in an effort to keep from clutching the steadily growing pain in her chest.

She wondered if Curt had figured out he'd picked someone as far away as possible from her own tomboy style. Ellen Ransom had a passion for pink. The woman made movie stars look overfed and underdressed.

"You said 'soon-to-be ex-wife?'" Flak drew the statement into a polite question.

"Well, that's kind of why we're out here." He paused, but Flak refused to help him out.

"I filed for divorce this morning. You'll be getting the papers pretty quick."

Flak bowed her head once more, and stared down at her short-clipped, unpainted fingernails in the merciful moonlight. She let out a breath that somehow felt like she'd been holding in for four years.

Four and a half, actually.

"Okay."

"That's all you got to say?"

"Yep."

"Then I guess…I guess I'll take you home."

"Sounds good."

Curt horsed the rattletrap truck around in a Y-turn complicated by the bridge abutment.

Once up on the road, and the loud thumping of the Angelina Bridge behind them, the knot in Flak's chest started to ease.

She got back to her own question at hand.

"Will Ellen sign a statement saying she was with you the night of the fire?"

"Well, she said she would, but she'd appreciate it if you'd keep it to yourself. At least until after the election."

"Shouldn't be a problem. Tell her to come see me when she can."

"You got it."

Curt pulled in her drive after the largely silent ride, put the gearshift in neutral, turned the motor off and set the brake.

Flak saw him begin to turn, and bent to tie her shoelace. It wasn't untied—she just didn't feel like looking at him right then.

As her head neared her knees, she heard the shattering crash of the truck's rear window, and the nearly simultaneous sound of a shot hard on its heels.

"Jesus Christ!" Curt shouted.

"Get down!" She reached over to yank his head into the seat, while pulling the rest of her own body into the floorboard.

She pulled her pistol out of its holster at the small of her back, checked the magazine by touch, and slid it back in with a harsh snap.

She felt along the dashboard, and found the hole just above the glove box, dead center of where her neck would have been.

"Stay down," she said to Curt in a rough whisper. "They have to be somewhere in the trees on the other side of the road. And a .22 might not punch through steel."

"How the hell do you know it's a .22?"

Before she thought, she said, "That's what they used to kill my dog."

"You found him?"

"They laid him on my back porch. Probably as a warning."

"Is this another warning?"

She shook her head. "No, I'm pretty sure they're serious now."

"Damn it."

"Yeah."

Silence.

The night creatures outside began to pick up their sounds again, tree frogs calling for rain, crickets.

Nothing rustling, no sound of movement. Through the absent back window, she could hear the wind rustling through the pines, and inside the truck, just the sound of Curt's breathing.

Flak wondered if his breathing was that loud before they split up, and if he quit smoking, if it would be quieter.

After what felt like hours of twitching her gaze back and forth from one window to the other to check for someone sneaking up to the truck, Flak said, "Look – give me your hat."

"What for?"

"Want to see if they're still out there."

"I don't want to get my hat shot up—I just bought it."

"It's better than getting your head shot up. Just give me the damn thing."

Curt handed her the baseball cap, keeping his body low.

"Stay still," she ordered.

"Yes ma'am. I got no desire for extra holes in my head."

Curt stayed on his side as Flak slithered over him. She dragged with her an old paintbrush she'd encountered with her toes earlier. Sticking it inside the cap, she inched it above the driver's seat.

She cursed under her breath at the porch light's glaring betrayal of their position, but hoped it flattened visibility enough to make the round cap look like someone's head peering over the back of the seat.

The hat did not draw a response, violent or otherwise. Slowly, she withdrew it.

"Are they gone?" Curt started to sit up, but Flak shoved him back down in the seat.

"Maybe. Let's try something else."

She moved back to the passenger side. As she neared Curt's head with hers, he suddenly kissed her.

She wiped her mouth with the back of her hand. "What the hell was for?"

"If I'm going to die, I wanted to kiss somebody. And you're the only woman in the truck."

"Oh, shut up."

"Okay."

The porch light showed Flak the white of his teeth bared in a grin. "Be still, damn it."

She slid upwards again, directly over Curt's head. She wasted one thought on hoping he was enjoying the proximity to her breasts. Survive or not, it was as close as he was ever going to get to them again. Even in the intensity of the moment, she realized the ache behind her breastbone was gone.

She turned the baseball cap around and slid it up slowly above the seat once more, hoping it looked like her head. If the killer was out for her alone, this should certainly draw fire. Again, no shot rang out.

She collapsed in slow motion back into the floorboard.

"Was it as good for you as it was for me, Neets?"

"Oh shut up, Curt."

"So, what now?" She took a moment's satisfaction from the fact he was finally asking her what to do instead of playing the man card.

But it was time to get moving instead of just sitting there waiting for the shooter to make the next move.

"Can you drive this bucket of rust without getting your head above the seat?"

"I can surely try."

She thought a moment. "Tell you what—you get the clutch with your right foot, and I'll crawl over you and unseat the parking brake once you get the truck started."

"I can't get the gas and the clutch from this angle."

"I'll get the gas, too. It shouldn't take much to goose us around the house. Just turn the wheel to make it about six feet left and then straighten it out, and we should be able to roll down into the back yard."

The precarious positions worked long enough to get the truck around the side of the house. As soon as Flak could see out the passenger window they were past the house, she yelled at Curt to make a hard right.

"Run for the house," she said, and bailed out the passenger side door with the truck still rolling.

Inside the back door of the darkened house, she went through every room, gun in hand, before picking up the phone.

"Dorrie—get Cliff out here to my house. Sirens, lights on. Now."

"You all right?" she asked her new floor ornament after she hung up. Curt lay exactly in the middle of the living room, hands holding his baseball cap at his chest, breath still coming in gasps.

"I could use a beer."

"Ain't got one, sorry."

A deep sigh from the man on the floor. "You do understand this is why I left, don't you?"

"Left where?"

"Left you."

"Oh." Flak thought for a few seconds. "You mean getting shot at, or not having any beer in the house?"

"Neither one."

"Then why?"

"A man wants to feel like a man in his own house, Flak."

The sound of the nickname was odd in his voice. She couldn't ever remember Curt using it before.

She stood by the edge of the picture window and pulled the curtain aside carefully. No sign of anyone—hostile or otherwise.

It took no effort to keep her voice free of emotion. All the pain was gone.

She took that deep breath she had been missing for so long. "I never tried to make you feel like less of a man, Curtis Lee."

His voice, too, held no anger or pain. "You didn't have to try."

"Then I'm sorry I wasn't what you wanted."

"Wanting had nothing to do with it. Hell, I never stopped wanting you. I still haven't," a depressed note sounded in his voice. "I popped a woody in the truck with you crawling all over me."

"Oh, well." Flak stomped down the satisfaction in her soul as being unworthy of a woman about to be divorced.

The sound of the siren preceded the flashing lights by a number of seconds.

"Time to get moving, bubba. I got work to do." She nudged him with the toe of her tennis shoe, and headed toward the door to give Clint instructions on how to do a perimeter search.

CHAPTER EIGHTEEN

Jenny

I don't remember when I started being aware he was watching me for something other than sheer meanness. I think I was more aware he was watching my older sister first. I caught her once putting towels over all the cracks in the bathroom and over the doorknob. The door had originally led outside, so it had a keyhole. I didn't tease her about it, and I teased her about almost everything. I didn't even ask her why she was doing it. I just knew.

The summer I was twelve was the worst for her, I think. At fourteen, my sister had developed early. Not a good thing in my family. He decides we're all going to the beach, so we load up the truck and we head down to Padre Island. Sounds like the Beverly Hillbillies pre-oil boom. Probably looked like it, too.

He must have just gotten paid for a job or something, because he spent money. He personally took charge of taking me and my sister to get bathing suits. He bought her a bikini, and tried to buy me one, but I pitched a quiet fit right there in the store and ended up with a swim dress instead.

Sis and I stayed in water up to our necks until we were wrinkly, then would get out and wrap up in towels. Drove him crazy. Didn't find out until later what was going on. Years later, she told me she'd been close to menopause during that trip, and was in the middle of what turned out to be like a sixty-day-long menstrual period.

So she stayed in long pants, long sleeves and a big sun hat the whole trip. She had the milk-white pale redhead skin that freckles easily and burns in ten seconds flat.

Between his sexual frustration, and some bizarre, warped sense of entitlement, my father was starting to pay attention to me and my sister that we were both extremely uncomfortable with.

He "tried out" his new Polaroid camera, this huge thing with metal struts and a kind of stretching bellows arrangement on the front, on me and my sister. The photos of me are all knees and elbows, pigtails and bony feet. He tried to make me pose like a movie star, but I looked like Olive Oyl.

My sister, bless her heart, was already way too "blessed." There's a euphemism for you. She could have passed for eighteen, easily, except for that look of bruised innocence on her face. Those pictures of my sister all disappeared. Still no idea what happened to them. In my memory, she was beautiful.

At first, the picture taking was better than being yelled at, or hit, but as it went on and on, it was just more terrorism in a different package. She caught it first, and I caught it worst. It wasn't her fault. He just got braver with me, that's all.

And you know what—it was the hardest thing of all. It sounds funny to say it, but it really did break my heart when I figured out he was a coward. It was like bravery was the only positive characteristic I could assign to him, you know?

All those years, I had two fathers in my head. One was smart and funny and a teacher. The other was mean and evil and nasty. But looking at it from my angle now, he only ever hurt people who couldn't hurt him back. Women and children, never anyone his own size.

Coward.

CHAPTER NINETEEN

Harley appeared in the office doorway. "Heard you got another bullet for me, boss."

Flak pitched the big deputy the evidence bag from her seat behind the desk.

"Do I get to know where you found this one?"

"We dug it out of Curtis Lee's dash last night. He was none too happy about it, either. Shot out his back window." Flak shook her head at the thought of someone caring more about their truck than their own safety.

Harley snorted. "Nobody is going to notice a little more duct tape on that ratty old truck."

Flak looked up, surprised. "You know his truck?"

Harley snorted. "Every woman in town knows that truck."

"Yeah, I'm sure they do." Flak looked down at the snowstorm of paper on her desk and kept adding to the piles of "to do," and "to put off."

Harley cleared her throat. Without looking at her, Flak said, "Thank you, Harley."

"No sweat, sheriff."

Flak continued stacking paper. The phone rang just as she found her desktop underneath it all.

"Sheriff speaking."

"Hey, girl, I hear somebody's been shooting at your butt."

She grinned. "Actually, Garv, they were shooting at my head. Smaller target. Probably why they missed."

"Anybody get hurt?"

"Only Curt's truck." She paused for a second and said what was on her mind. "And his ego, it turns out."

Garvey's slow drawl deepened even further. "Speaking of that particular devil, I also read this morning he filed for divorce."

"Read where?"

"In the legal actions column in the paper. Don't you get the Daily Sentinel?"

"Yeah, but I didn't get a chance to read it this morning. Crap, crap, crap." Flak sat back in her chair. Now everybody in town would be gossiping about her again.

"Well, that's kind of what I called about. Are you okay? With the divorce, I mean."

She didn't answer the question directly. "Well, I did know he was going to file. That's what he came out to tell me last night. Getting shot at kind of shifted the topic of conversation."

"Yeah, I can see that."

Silence reigned on both ends of the line for a few moments.

Garvey broke first. "How about I bring dinner out tonight."

"It's Tuesday!"

"So?"

"So you only bring dinner out on Fridays."

"Well, it could just be I've got a date Friday night."

"With who?"

"None of your dang business." Flak could hear Garvey's grin in the words.

She didn't like the way the conversation was going. "Seriously, man. Why tonight?"

Garvey switched directions on her. "Did you ever find that mutt of yours?"

"Noooo." Flak drew the word out into a question. She didn't want to tell him Barney was dead, not when anybody walking by her office could hear.

"Then how about I come out and bark at anybody who tries to shoot you."

Flak did not like the way this conversation was heading at all. "So you're volunteering for bodyguard."

"Just 'til folks stop trying to perforate you."

"I'm the sheriff. Somebody's mad at me all the time."

"Usually they take their potshots in the Sound Off column in the paper, not at your head."

She didn't have an answer for that. "Look. You can bring dinner, but you can't stay. With the notice in the paper this morning, there's going to be way too many people gossiping as it is."

"Fine. I'll be there."

"Eight o'clock?"

"Why don't we make it seven," he said, "since it's a work night."

"I'm easy."

"I'm hoping." He hung up.

Flak contemplated the silent receiver for a moment and placed it back in its cradle.

She pulled out the timeline she'd created the day before and went back through the sequence showing the events before and after Tucker's death one more time. Still holding it, she picked up the phone and dialed Garvey back.

"Chief Garvey."

"Hey, it's me."

"You can't cancel on me now; you already agreed I'd bring dinner."

"No that ain't it," she said. "This is business."

"Ok, then, what's up?"

"When exactly was that fire at the Looneyville store?"

"Somewhere around late April, early May."

"No," she explained. "I need an actual date."

"Sure. Hang on just a second." She heard the receiver click on his desk and the sound of a metal file drawer rolling open.

Moments later, she heard the sound of papers flipping. "Let's see. It was April 30."

Flak marked the date into her timeline. "How bad was it, exactly?"

She heard a creak, and pictured Garvey leaning back in the beat-up old chair he favored. When he answered her, she could tell he had his pipe clenched in his teeth. He never lit it at work, but he carried it around like a dog with a ratty old bone.

"It was just kid stuff. Somebody set fire to a bunch of cardboard boxes. It took out part of the back wall and ceiling."

"Why would it send those folks packing?"

"The Taylors? Don was looking for any excuse to pull Sara back out of there. He told everybody in the county he was a city boy and he missed it. Personally, I don't think he liked getting his hands dirty."

"So the fire was just a good excuse for them to go back home?"

"That's what it seemed like to me. They didn't have any insurance to speak of, so it wasn't about that. Why you interested?"

"Just the timing mostly. Look, man, I gotta get off this phone. I'll see you later." It took her three tries to get the phone back on the cradle while she mentally poked and pried at the information in the sequence of events.

A clear evidence bag holding a bullet suddenly appeared in her doorway, dangled at the end of Harley's meaty fingers.

"Yes?"

"Same gun, boss." Harley's head caught up with her hand in the opening.

"Did you check to see if any of Miz Emlyn's kids had a .22 registered?"

Harley answered the question with her own. "You think one of them's shooting at you?"

"Well, Curtis had a good alibi," Flak said without allowing the smile to make it to her lips. "But I'm going to need you to check on the rest. Any luck on checking the gun registration?"

"Nope. Sorry, but an ungodly number of weapons in the state aren't registered. That run on guns before the Brady law took effect, remember?"

"I hadn't forgotten," Flak murmured, still trying to will the timeline to give up more information.

"You need anything else from me, Sheriff?"

"No. Wait—yes. Get in touch with Garrison Oil. See if you can get Frederick Miller's schedule since the beginning of April. When was he out, what sites he was at, when was he at home. And see if you can find out whether Garrison received samples of a missile fuel to put in a bid to Kindjal Industries."

Harley tucked the evidence bag in her pocket and scribbled the particulars on her hand. "What else?"

"Get a dang notebook, would you?"

The big deputy grinned at Flak. "I always lose 'em. I can usually find my hand when I need it."

"Shoo." Flak ordered, pointing the way.

"Yes'm."

A few hours later, Flak got paper plates from one kitchen cabinet and plastic cups from another to use for iced tea. She put them on the counter in front of her, and lost track of time for a minute, still trying to figure out which of Curt's brothers and sisters could have been shooting at her a mere twenty-four hours prior. Garvey's voice made her jump and whirl around. "I see we're using the good china."

"Dang it, I'm not going to get shot between the living room and the kitchen. Would you quit following me around?"

He made calm-down motions with his hands. "Man, you're jumpy! I was just wondering what took so long."

"Oh." She looked down at the paper goods in front of her. "I just keep losing track of where I am today; trying to get this Barnes thing sorted out."

He shook his head, clicked his tongue. "Got to learn to leave it at work, girl."

"That's kind of tough when somebody shoots your dog and then tries to kill you, too."

"Excuse me?"

She looked at him, drawing himself up to his full height, and his face starting to redden. "Oh, crap. Look, Garv, I didn't mean to say anything about it yet. You got to keep it quiet."

"Keep what quiet." His tone of voice demanded an answer.

"Look…"

"Stop telling me to 'look,' girl. I like what I'm looking at, but I do not like what I'm hearing." He was shaking his head as he moved toward her, and she took a step back.

"Well, if you're going to get all crazy on me, I ain't telling you nothing."

Garvey grabbed her arm and pulled her toward the kitchen table. After a few reluctant steps, she yanked it out of his grasp.

"Stop it, Garv. Right now. You can calm down or you can leave."

"Fine." Flak could tell the single word had cost him. He took a seat at the table, then a few deep breaths.

"Sheriff Anders, would you like to take a seat?" He waved her to the chair across from him.

"Thank you, no; I believe I'll stand." She matched his formal tone.

"Would you care to tell me what the hell is going on?"

"Not if you're going to act like some stupid redneck." She folded her arms and looked him dead in the eye.

"No promises." He bared his teeth at her.

"Then no answers." Flak turned toward the living room. A second later, Garvey's hand on her arm spun her around like a child's top. She swung her outside fist around with the rotation and caught him right in the chin with an uppercut. It was like hitting a brick wall.

She shook her hand from the stinging pain. Garv didn't sway a single inch from the blow, but he let her go.

"Do you feel better now?" he asked in a much calmer tone than before.

"A little bit," she admitted.

"Good. *Now* would you like to tell me what happened to your dog?"

"Um. Sure."

Garvey walked to the kitchen table, not even looking back to see if she followed.

Flak took a moment to put together two iced teas, put one in front of Garvey, and took a seat across from him.

As she told the fire chief about finding Barney dead on her back step, she rubbed her battered knuckles in the condensed moisture on the outside of her glass. The pain in her hand helped distract her from the content of the conversation. She fully intended to keep her tears to herself, but couldn't help the occasional pause and painful swallow.

Garvey shifted in his chair only once, when she mentioned Doc Adams' theory that someone had placed the dog's body there as a warning.

"Did the bullets match?" was his first question.

"Yep, pretty much. The one we found at the scene of Tucker Barnes's fire, and now the one from last night." She pulled one shoulder up in a half shrug. "Not great, though. You know how messed up .22 slugs get from impact. Might hold up in court, might not."

"So you got one shooter."

"Not necessarily," she objected. "We got one gun. For all I know, three different people could have pulled the trigger. They're a close family. Too close for comfort."

"You think one of Miz Emlyn's kids did all this?"

Flak nodded. "They're my primary suspects. Curtis Lee's the only one that's got an alibi for last night and his dad's murder, but he was alone the night Barney was killed. There's not a single night all five of them have reliable witnesses to say they were somewhere else." She lapsed into silence, looking down at her hands.

While Curtis Lee's affair with the mayor's wife might give him a good alibi for Tucker's death, as well, she had promised to keep his secret.

Deep in her own thoughts, it took her a while to realize Garvey hadn't responded. She raised her head and met his eyes.

The bushy, salt-and-pepper eyebrows above his clear blue eyes crimped in the middle as he frowned at her. "Why don't I just stay out here with you for a while, then?"

"Nope. Uh-uh. No way." She shook her head side to side with each negative. "Gossips are already having a field day with my life."

"I don't give a rat's rear-end about gossip."

"You're not an elected official. I am. Plus, I wouldn't put it past this nutbag to set a fire somewhere to toll you out of here."

"You got a point there." Garvey sat back in his chair and stroked his chin.

"I'm not sure they'll try again anyway."

"And what little birdie told you that?"

"Just instinct." Flak continued soothing her bruised knuckles on the chilly cup, and contemplated the melting ice.

"The same instinct nearly got you perforated last night?"

Flak rose to get more ice. "The key word there is 'nearly.' I ain't dead yet."

With her head and upper body shielded by the freezer door, she buried her aching hand in the ice bin.

Still breathing in the frigid air curling around her, "Hey, Garv?"

"Yeah?"

"Why didn't you hit me back?"

Only silence from the man at the kitchen table. She waited. He finally mumbled something.

She snagged a handful of ice and added it to her cup, then refilled it with tea. At the table once more, she looked him in the face.

"I didn't quite catch that. What did you say?"

"I said, 'I ain't sure it was actually me you were swinging at.'"

"My busted knuckles and the red spot on your chin say otherwise."

He threw up his hands.

"Oh hell, girl, I ain't never hit no woman, and I dang sure ain't going to start with you."

"So it's a sexist thing?"

"No, by God, it's not."

"Then what?"

Garvey shouted, "I didn't hit you because I love you."

CHAPTER TWENTY

Jenny

Look, if you want to get your jollies by hearing about incest and rape, go talk to somebody else. You ain't going to hear it from me. In order to tell the gory details, you have to relive it, and I have no intentions of going back there anytime soon.

Ever, if I can help it.

I laughed myself sick the first time I heard about suppressed memory syndrome. You know the one where a shrink brings up memories some person, usually a woman, has hidden even from herself about being raped as a child.

Now that is one condition I prayed for, literally, on my knees. Just let me forget. But I can't.

What I can do, and what I have to do in order to keep standing upright, is just push them to side. It's necessary for me to get on with my life. So, I have no great urge to relive those incidents with you.

Yes, he raped me. More than once. You already know that.

What you don't know is what it did inside my head—that's harder to explain than the physical stuff, anyway.

Bruises heal, scars fade, but the rest... Well, you walk through your days on automatic. When somebody says, "go here," you go, you don't ask questions. When no one tells you to do anything, you just stand there, like a mechanical doll without batteries.

I hate dolls.

There's not enough water in the entire world to wash the feeling off the outside of you, and the inside of you is like just-made gelatin. Weak and trembly and scared.

My sister told me, long after, she had met her boyfriend under the pine tree out in front of our house one dark night and gave him her virginity. It was the one thing she had that our father wanted that she had some control over.

I wasn't quick enough or smart enough or old enough to think of it, but I wish I had.

CHAPTER TWENTY-ONE

Flak was still thinking about Garvey's revelation two days later. She hadn't known how to respond, so she just changed the subject, dished up dinner, and got him out of the house as quick as she could. It had been a silent, tense meal.

She sighed and went back to the timeline she had propped up on her desk against the piles of paper. She kept going back to the Looeyville store fire.

It was just too handy—Emlyn Barnes' kids hadn't all been in East Texas at the same time for four years. Since her funeral in fact. Now here they all were, and Tucker Barnes just happened to die in a suspicious fire.

Harley tapped on her door frame, came into her office and sat gingerly in the chair across from her. Flak pushed the timeline aside and put her elbows on the desk, arms folded.

"What you got?"

"Well, your ex-husband-to be is the only one with a good alibi for the night you got shot at."

The big deputy thumbed through the papers. "Let's see... Maggie Kovax and Jenny Samuels are each other's alibi again."

Flak nodded.

"Ben Campbell says he was at his home in Lufkin practicing his songs. No neighbors close enough to confirm."

"And Frederick?"

"Well, here's where it gets interesting. His wife says he's at work. The folks at Garrison Oil say he's not due back at work until September 1. August is his off month."

"So where is he?"

"Nobody seems to know."

"Did you try to get a contact phone for him?"

Harley nodded, but then immediately shook her head.

"No joy. Garrison says he's got a cell phone in his company truck, but it's being used by somebody else. It always is during his off month."

"Did you talk to his wife?"

Nodding again, Harley said, "Yeah, and that's one I won't soon forget. That is not a nice lady."

"Did you tell her he wasn't at work?"

"Nope, just said we were trying to get in touch with him to ask him some questions. She said he was at work and not to call back. Among a few other things Jesus probably would not have said."

Flak sat back, grabbed a pen and started tapping it on her desk in time with her thoughts. "You did good, Harley. While you were on the phone with Garrison, did you ask them about the fuel from Kindjal?"

"Yep. They said they got it, and they're working on the sample now to put together a proposal for manufacture."

Flak dropped the pen, leaned back in her chair and put her hands behind her head. "Okay, so Miller should have been working in July, May and March, going back."

Harley looked at her notes, "Yep."

"All right. I need one more thing from you, Harl. Find out where all the brothers and sisters were the night of April 30."

Harley sighed. "All five of them?"

Flak gave a sharp nod. "Yep."

Once the big deputy was out of her office, Flak felt like she could take a deep breath again. Harley's frame filled up a small room with little air to spare.

Flak added the information on Frederick's whereabouts to her painstaking timeline. After staring at it a few more minutes, she grabbed her hat. Standing, she settled it firmly on her head.

As she walked out to the cruiser parked in the spot marked "County Sheriff," she forcibly removed Garvey from her thoughts. She'd have to decide what to do about him sooner or later, but at the moment, later was fine with her.

The drive out to the Looneyville store soothed her soul. Swooping curves melted under the cruiser's wheels like butter in the summer heat as she listened with one ear to the usual rattle of radio traffic. The only sight that marred the pleasant drive was the proliferation of crosses and flowers along the roadside. Each marked a death at that spot on the road, and it seemed no long stretch was without them. While Flak understood the need for the families to memorialize their loved ones, it was, nonetheless, disturbing.

The now-white building gleamed in the morning sunshine. Flak had to shield her eyes from the glare until she got up under the canopy.

No one answered her knock, so she went around the side of the store building to the trailer and tried there.

"Hello, Anita—you look very official today," Jenny said after she opened the door. "Come on in—you want some tea?"

"Sure."

Flak took off her Stetson and entered the pretty little trailer. It was immaculate.

She sniffed the air. "Something smells good."

"Cookies. Maggie thinks baking is good therapy, so she's got me slaving away."

"Baking always made me nervous." Flak sat on the flowered couch with her hat in her hands. "All that measuring and waiting."

"Here you go." Jenny handed her a tinkling glass. Flak took it with one hand, and placed the Stetson carefully on its crown on the couch beside her.

"Thanks. Is Maggie here?"

"Nope, just us loonies." Jenny perched on the edge of the loveseat a few steps away, elbows on her knees, both hands clutching her own glass, and gave Flak her undivided attention.

"So what can I do for you?" The look in her eyes was intent, even a little unnerving.

"You up to answering some questions?"

"Sure, why not?" Jenny looked at the glass she held as she turned it in her fingers.

At Flak's hesitation, she said, "Oh, Maggie's given you the whole speech, right? Jenny's too fragile; Jenny's too weak to deal with the real world."

Flak nodded. "Something like that, yeah."

"Maggie protects me because she feels guilty for leaving. That's what the shrink said, anyway. I prefer to believe it's because she loves me, but what do I know?"

She paused. "Ask what you need to ask, Sheriff. I won't promise that I won't flip out, but I'll try to warn you before I run amok, okay?"

Flak had no answer, so filled the empty space with a question. "When Frederick drove up Saturday, you vanished. Why?"

Jenny shrugged. "I guess I'm not ready to be cried over, that's all. I can only stand so many 'poor babies.' Maggie protects me, but she doesn't pity me."

"Was that the only reason?"

"That and the fact that Raylene makes me want to put an ice pick through both eardrums. Deafness is a blessing around that woman. Lately, she's decided we need to go to the county garage sales. She wakes us up every Friday and Saturday morning and drags us off to Nacogdoches with her."

Jenny shuddered. "It's like a whole morning's preview of hell."

Flak smiled. "I can't disagree with you there."

They both sipped their tea. Flak made an involuntary face at the sweet taste.

Jenny's intent eyes must have caught the expression. "You want some unsweet? Won't take but a minute."

"No, that's okay." Flak waved her back to her seat. "Just wasn't ready for it."

"You sure?"

"Yeah, thanks. Look, Jenny. Do you know what Maggie does for a living?"

"I know she's a consultant."

"What does she consult on?"

Jenny laughed. "You know, I got my head far enough out of my own butt one time to ask her, and she said she could tell me, but she'd have to kill me."

Flak grunted.

"That's a yolk, son," Jenny pointed out. "But if you really want to know, you can ask her. I believe she just drove up."

Maggie came through the door loaded for bear. "I thought I told you to leave Jenny alone."

"It's okay, Mags," the younger woman said, reaching a hand toward her sister.

"No, it's not." Maggie advanced a few more steps toward the couch. If she'd been a cat, Flak figured, her fur would be fluffed out and she'd be spitting already.

Jenny rose. She might have been only two inches taller than her angry sibling, but her voice was several decibels louder. "Yes, it is okay."

Maggie turned to look at her sister, and all the fight in her seemed to drain away.

"Jen, I'm just trying…"

"I know what you're 'just trying,' and I'm telling you it's all right. Truly."

"But…"

"Stop it. Sit down. Here, drink my tea. I'll bring you a damn cookie." Jenny marched into the kitchen.

Maggie sat in the spot Jenny had vacated and watched her sister move around the kitchen. Flak watched her as well.

Back in the living room, Jenny shoved a cookie into Maggie's hand and silently offered one to Flak, who shook her head.

"Now. I'm going to go dust something in the store." Jenny looked directly into her sister's eyes. "And you are going to answer the nice sheriff's questions. Got it?"

"Right," Maggie said faintly, and nibbled the cookie.

Jenny went out the trailer door and closed it gently behind her.

Maggie hung her head. "I'm sorry, Anita, I just…"

"I understand."

"Do you?"

"I think so. But I also think she needs less protection every day."

Silence fell. For once, Flak figured she better break it. She wanted to catch Maggie a little off balance.

"What did you do for Kindjal Industries, Maggie?"

"It's top secret," she muttered, looking at the door Jenny had exited.

"I don't want details, just vague outlines will do."

"I worked as a chemical engineering consultant."

"Did you work on missile fuels?"

"Yes," Maggie said, drawing out the word. Her full attention returned to Flak.

"Did you have access to the fuel samples they created for the kinetic energy missile program?"

The surprise on Maggie's face was obvious. "How do you know about that?"

"It doesn't matter."

"Why are you asking about all this?"

"Because one of those samples may have been used to set the fire that killed your father."

"Oh my God."

"Did you have access to those samples, Maggie?"

Maggie's fingers covered her mouth, as if trying to hold the words in. She nodded.

"Do you have them now?"

Maggie shook her head, fingers still trapping her thoughts.

"Who does?" Flak urged her to speak.

"I'm the one who made it happen. I talked Kindjal into letting Garrison bid for the contract."

"Who got the samples, Maggie?" Flak figured she knew as soon as the other woman mentioned Garrison, but she wanted to hear her say it.

"Frederick."

The horror on Maggie's face was hard to look at. Was she acting? If she was, she was one of the best Flak had ever seen.

She reassured the stricken woman as best she could. "Look. Just because Frederick had a sample at one point doesn't mean he did this. Garrison says he delivered a sample to them."

Maggie shook her head hard, over and over again. "That's just it, though. It wasn't just one sample. There were three."

Flak could feel her mouth drop open. "You're joking."

Maggie shook her head again. "No. Three samples in divided glass containers about so big." She placed her fingers six inches apart. About the size of a soda can.

"Why glass? And why three samples?"

"The chemicals react with each other and with any organic substance, including plastic. It was either steel or glass."

She didn't answer the second question, but Flak decided to leave it for the moment.

"Okay. Let's think about this. We know Garrison actually did get a sample. We know one or more were used on Tucker's house."

"Only one, if the fuel sample was your fire source." Maggie's voice assumed a clipped, professional tone. "Two of them would have taken out more than half a city block."

"Rough stuff."

Maggie shrugged. "It has to be to fuel these missiles."

"I need to know a couple other things, too."

"Shoot."

Flak asked, "Did you take Frederick the samples before or after his birthday?"

"Neither. He picked them up in Dallas in mid-May."

"Why? Why couldn't you take them to him?"

"Company policy."

Flak rose and started pacing, trying to fit what she was getting from Maggie around the timeline she pictured in her head. "When were you done with your contract with Kindjal?"

"About the same time."

"When did you find out about the store being up for sale?"

"About the fifth or sixth of May."

"You said Frederick called you about it, right?"

Maggie nodded once more. "Yeah—that's when I told him the samples would be ready for him on the fifteenth."

"What did he say about the store?"

"Just that the people who were running it had decided to go back to Austin."

"Did he say why?"

"No." Maggie paused. "Why do you want to know?"

"When did you find out about the fire damage?"

"Not until I came down to look at it in mid-June."

"What did Frederick say about it?"

"I don't remember details—just something about kids and the temptation of empty buildings. Why?"

"I'm not sure you want to hear it."

"What could be worse than my brother being suspected of murder?" Maggie sipped her tea, put it on a coaster on the end table and wiped her damp hands on her jeans.

"How close are you to Frederick?"

"Not as close as I am to Jenny."

"That's not an answer."

"That's all I've got."

Flak slid her thumbs in her pants pockets. She faced the other woman. "How do I know you're telling the truth about the samples?"

Maggie shrugged. If the question irritated her, she didn't let it show. "You don't, I guess."

"Did you have any of the samples in your possession?"

"No, Never. I helped develop the fuel itself—but the only way to get physical samples out of the plant was to sign them out as an authorized representative of one of the bidding companies. That's why Frederick had to come to Dallas to get them."

"How do I know you didn't get one back from him afterward? Or two?"

"You don't," Maggie said quietly. "But I assure you, I did not."

Flak simply stood there and looked at her.

"Sheriff, I have an IQ well above 160. I graduated top of my class. I am on hiatus at the moment from a thriving consulting career. I have a husband who loves me. What in that list makes you think I'd risk it all to kill an old man for his thirty-year-old sins?"

By the time Maggie was done, she stood nose-to-nose with Flak, though she had to jut her chin out to do so.

"Curt was wrong," Flak said. "You do know how to defend yourself."

"Is that what I'm doing?" Maggie retired once more to the love seat. "Do I need a lawyer?"

"No," Flak said thoughtfully. "But Frederick probably will. One last question, Maggie. Curt's letter was sent in March. Did you talk to Ben or Frederick about it?"

"Yes—both of them called me."

"Do you still have the letter?"

Maggie shook her head. "Not with me. It's at my house up north."

"Can I get a copy?"

"I'll get my husband to send it to you. Give me your fax number." Maggie handed Flak the pen and notepad from the table.

Jenny walked in, but rather than stopping, just moved on into the kitchen. "Do you want some lunch, Sheriff?"

"No. No thanks. I think it's time I got back into town. Maggie—can you walk me to the car?"

"Sure. Back in a sec, Jen."

"Take your time." Jenny waved them out the door.

"So. You going to tell me what's going through your head?" Maggie asked as they walked across the parking lot.

"Not all of it."

"What you can, then."

Flak took a deep breath. "Frederick lied to you. The fire here wasn't set after the owners left. It was actually what convinced them to go. I think he might have set it, but I can't prove it. Yet."

"Oh." Maggie stumbled over a large piece of gravel. "But why?"

"He wanted you here for some reason."

Maggie's baffled look matched Flak's own confusion.

Flak pulled open the door of her cruiser. "Look, Maggie, if he calls, don't say anything. I'm going to see if we can dig him up, get him in for questioning and see if this is all just a big flap about nothing."

Maggie shook her head. "It's just insane, that's all. Frederick was the only one of us who got along with Tucker. He was the son Tucker wanted, even though he was someone else's blood."

"One last question," the sheriff said, "Why three samples, why not just one?"

"Oh, I'm sorry, I meant to tell you. Frederick said Garrison had three labs that were going to work on it—there are a number of different components, and their labs are specialized. Or at least, that's what he told me."

Flak nodded. "We'll find out, but I have a feeling that was just a way to get more than one sample."

The sheriff touched the other woman's arm, not something she would usually do, but Maggie's face had lost all color. "For yours and Jenny's safety, Maggie, don't say anything. To anybody. There's still one sample of missile fuel out there. And it's walking around with someone who's obviously not afraid to use it."

Maggie nodded. Arms wrapped around her body, she looked like she was freezing in the summer heat. She was still there in Flak's rearview mirror as the sheriff took the left turn for Nacogdoches.

CHAPTER TWENTY-TWO

Jenny

His "magnificent obsession," he called it. "That damned boat" is what Mama called it, though certainly not in his hearing. Until the day she died, she wouldn't even hang a picture of a boat on a wall.

The other fascination my father developed in my twelfth summer, besides having sex with me and my sister, was building a boat. In the middle of seventy-something acres of prime timber, more than a hundred miles from the nearest open water, he began building an eighteen-foot, oceangoing sloop.

Seriously.

Unless you'd been there, you cannot begin to understand the complexity of building something that big with just your hands. Actually, with just our hands. Our father directed the work while we built. Everything in our lives was forced to take second place to his dream. As the framework rose, it became the backdrop to every fight, every torture, to our entire lives.

In 1973, the pump on the well gave out. By that time, every cent he made was going toward building the boat. There was no way he would spend money to replace the pump, so from then on, we drew water out of the well. I was so small I couldn't let the two-gallon bucket fill all the way up, or it would drag me down with it.

The rope was covered with ice in the winter time, as well. Saying it was a pain is understatement of the highest caliber. Mama boiled some for drinking and cooking water every day, and we used the rest for the toilet and for baths. Why did she boil it? Because the old man decided one of the cats that disappeared must have fallen down the well and died, so we had to boil everything we drank after that decision.

Did you know you can pour two or three gallons of water down the toilet bowl and it will flush automatically?

By 1975, the boys were out on their own, so their room became a machine shop. He bought every tool known to man on credit from Sears, Roebuck. That's how we found out he was even creepier than we thought he was.

He was using the table saw, and took off half of his thumb, the long way, right down through the thumbnail. The bone was showing. He made my sister patch it up for him, probably because I was making puking noises. It looked like raw hamburger meat. After about two years, it grew back. Swear to God.

Mama spent days sewing canvas drop cloths together to make a giant tent for his baby, and we helped him build an A-frame to support the tent. Then we built the bulkheads, the entire frame, and the keel. No power tools for that, just me and my mother and my sister with hand-held screwdrivers. Blisters eventually became calluses on our hands.

Mama convinced him to kick us out eventually. If our leaving had been anything but his idea, he would have killed both of us. By that time, he had kicked my sister out of the house, with a four-ten shotgun pointed at her head.

He left after we did, and the skeleton of the boat stayed there. I heard later someone hooked a tractor to it and dragged it further down in the woods. This was after they'd blunted a couple of axes on it trying to cut it up for firewood. I could have told them an axe wouldn't cut through the thousands of screws and gallons of epoxy we used to build it.

I'm sure it's still down there in the woods—it won't rot for hundreds of years, if then. But East Texas does reclaim anything if left long enough. I am sure the frame is now covered with devil vines and poison ivy. Small animals probably make their homes in the safe place created, literally, with our blood, sweat and tears. There's some satisfaction in that thought.

CHAPTER TWENTY-THREE

Flak arrived at her office to find the building nearly empty. She looked at her watch. Yep, lunchtime.

At her desk, she added the dates Maggie had given her to the timeline. She was about to start putting together a faxed APB when she realized she had no idea what Frederick was driving. She tabled it for the moment and put together a description without vehicle information.

Talking to Raylene was a task she planned to put off as long as she possibly could.

She handed the sheet over to the day dispatcher with strict instructions to keep it off the radio. She didn't want Curt to hear over the police band that his brother was being sought for questioning.

By the time she'd taken care of all that, workers trickled back in from their lunchtime destinations.

Flak caught Harley in the hallway.

"Where's Cliff's report on Monday night's shooter?"

"I can get it for you, but all he came up with was a few scuff marks on a low branch and a shell, no print."

"Thanks." Flak said, and hurried into her office to catch the ringing phone.

"Hey girl, you had lunch?"

"Nope."

"Why don't you meet me over at Casa Tomas. My treat."

She shook her head, more at herself than the man on the phone. "I don't know, Garv."

"You gotta eat."

She patted her too-tight uniform pants. "I could stand to skip a meal or two."

"Come on, Flak—no strings, just lunch."

She gave in. "Okay, okay, I'll meet you there in fifteen minutes."

"See you."

Flak wasn't sure she was ready to see Garvey yet, but she did want to ask him if that was his car she'd seen drift by her house late Tuesday night and Wednesday night, too. While she appreciated the thought, it felt like she was under surveillance.

When she arrived, the lunchtime crowd was nearly gone. Three of the tiny Philippina nurses from Memorial Hospital, identifiable by their colorful smocks and white comfortable shoes, chattered at a table near the wall. Garvey sat near the entrance in the open room, and lifted one hand in greeting. The smells of chili powder and sizzling meats made her mouth water. When had she eaten last? She couldn't remember.

She pulled the chair out across from the chief and turned the volume down on her radio until it was a crackling whisper.

"Hey, Flak," the waitress said as she put down two glasses of tea. She had two menus tucked under elbow, but didn't bother to hand them over.

"Thanks, Gretchen. I'll take the number four lunch plate."

"You got it. Chief?"

The big man across the table rumbled, "The same for me."

"Two cheese enchilada plates out in just a minute, y'all."

Flak toyed with her glass. For the first time she could remember, she felt unsure of what to say to Garvey.

"How's your hand, girl?" Flak involuntarily glanced at her scraped-up knuckles.

"Better than it was. How's your chin?"

"Oh, tolerable. I been hit harder."

She could hear the smile in his voice, and finally met his eyes. It was time to find out more about this man that said he loved her.

"You know what, Garvey, I was trying to remember what your first name was, and I realized I'd never heard it. Even when you stood up with Mary, the preacher called you 'I.R. Garvey.'"

"Yeah, I asked him to especially for me. I'm surprised Mary never told you."

Flak smiled. "I never asked her. So, what is your first name?"

He shook his head. "It's I.R."

"Come on. What's your name?"

He sighed. "My given name is Ignatius. The 'R' stands for Royal."

Flak had to swallow fast to keep from laughing her mouthful of tea right out on the table. "Excuse me?"

"You heard it right. I ain't saying it again."

"Did your mama hate you?"

"No," Garv said, resigned to a question he'd obviously heard before. "But she loved her Uncle Iggy, so she named me after him."

"Iggy. Really." Flak's grin was beginning to hurt her face, so she stared down at her tea again and struggled to control it.

"Yep. She's the only one who still calls me that."

Flak used the time-worn phrase Texans use when all else fails. "Well, bless your heart."

"I don't tell most people." He reached one long arm across the table, lifted her chin with his hand and exposed the smile she couldn't suppress. "And that possum grin is exactly why. So keep it to yourself."

"I promise," Flak crossed her heart. "Not sure anybody would believe me, anyway."

"Any progress on your shooter?" Garvey reclaimed his hand to spread his napkin on his lap, and dug into the fragrant food Gretchen had placed in front of him.

"Yeah. I might have a suspect."

Garv motioned with his fork for her to keep going.

"You told me the night of the fire you had dated Maggie Barnes a couple times, right?"

At his nod, "Did you know her older brother, Frederick?" Flak took a moment to get a bite of her own enchiladas.

Garvey's forehead creased, concentrating. "Yeah, a little. We used to play scrimmages with them for practice. Frederick's team went to region one year, as far as they ever got, and he was a big reason."

Flak nodded, and swallowed before she spoke. "Yeah, Curt told me he played football."

"Frederick's your shooter?"

"It's looking like he might be. Did you talk to Jim about the accelerant in the fire that killed Tucker?"

"A little bit. You seemed like you had it under control, and I didn't want to step on your toes. I just kept up with what was going on."

Flak looked at him in amazement. Any other Texan male public servant would have elbowed her out of the way without a thought.

She shook off the notion. "Well, it's possible Frederick had a fuel sample with that chemical signature in his hands. In fact, it's possible he still has at least one more."

"That don't sound good."

"I just put out an APB on him. I'd like to get him into custody and get some answers to a whole bunch of questions. Like, for instance, if he set your fire out at the Looneyville store."

Garvey spoke around a mouthful. "What makes you think he did?"

"He lied to Maggie about when it happened, for no earthly reason either one of us can figure out. There's something still missing on that one."

Garvey shook his head. "Don't sound like the Frederick I knew. He was always a straight shooter. If you'll pardon the expression."

"Did you know the rest of them?"

"Pretty much. I was a little too old to know Jenny well. She was a couple of years down from me in age. The rest? Yeah I know 'em. Why?"

"Did you know every one of them can shoot? And if you did, why didn't you tell me?"

Garvey shrugged. "Every country kid I ever met knew their way around a gun. You grew up in the city, didn't you?"

"Yeah, near Dallas—came down here to Stephen F. Austin for a criminal justice degree."

"If you'd grown up here, it wouldn't surprise you. Country kids are raised around guns. If you want to keep them from blowing their little brothers or sisters out of the water, you have to show them how they work, how to shoot and how to be safe with them."

Flak went back to her subject. "Did Maggie ever tell you when you were dating whether Tucker was abusing her and Jenny?"

She took another bite of her food, and realized she hadn't gotten an answer. When she looked at Garvey, he looked completely shocked.

She went on, "I'm not absolutely sure of that, but all the signs are there. Did she ever say anything?"

Garv shook his head. "I knew Maggie was… I don't know, brittle somehow. I didn't know why, and at nineteen years old, I was too stupid to ask."

"She's not brittle anymore. She's a tough cookie, and would fight bears for her little sister."

His eyes were focused on something only he could see, from twenty years past, maybe. While she had him reeling a bit, she figured she might as well keep going.

"Also, about Tuesday night."

That brought his focus back to the table in a hurry. His face took on a poker player's flat expression.

"While I genuinely appreciate your effort, I don't want you driving past my house every hour on the hour all night long."

He smiled at her, "I have no idea…."

"Ignatius Royal Garvey, don't you lie to me."

He flinched. "I never should have told you that."

"I mean it, Garvey."

Nodding, "I know you do."

"I'm not some helpless little girl needs protecting."

"You got it all wrong, Flak. I wasn't out there protecting you—I was trying to protect the poor criminal that killed your dog. He ain't figured out who he's messing with."

She leveled the old evil eye at him.

"All right, okay. I'll leave you alone to get your butt shot off."

She laughed. "Look, I got to get moving. I need to talk to Curt."

At Garvey's raised eyebrow, "I don't want him catching wind from some old busybody or from the radio that we're hunting for Frederick. I owe him that much."

Garvey threw both hands up, "I didn't say nothing about nothing."

"Uh-huh. I gotta go."

"We still on for Friday? I'll bring Chinese."

"Under one condition. That I don't see your ugly mug patrolling my house between now and then."

She could see the wheels turning behind Garvey's eyes. But all he said was, "You will not see my ugly mug patrolling your house between now and then. I swear."

Flak stood to leave, but sat back down. She pasted the most serious expression she could muster on her face. "There is one more condition."

Garvey looked at her with deep suspicion in his expression. "What's that?"

"You have to remember the dern fortune cookies—you forgot 'em last time."

"That's enough smart mouth out of you for one day, girl. Git."

"Yes, sir."

Flak walked into the parking lot still smiling. She knew she hadn't brought up that big old declaration of love he'd laid on her, but she had plenty of time.

Stopping by the office, she checked the fax machine, but nothing yet from Maggie's husband. Now the question was how she could find Curtis Lee. He'd never carried a cell phone—often didn't answer his home phone.

She pointed the car up Main Street, and felt the familiar vibrations caused by the uneven old brick streets through the steering wheel of the cruiser. The antiques district was mildly crowded with the last of the summer shoppers. She made a full circuit of the square, more for the pleasure of it than any other reason, and then continued east to University Drive.

If she remembered right, the paint store north of Medical Center, near where University met the Loop, was where he usually hung out. If he wasn't there, they would probably know where she could find him.

After she'd gotten the information she needed, Flak hit the Loop again and drove around the southeast side of town, amusing herself by scaring the dog out of the speeders. While stopping them was within the scope of her responsibilities, she felt too lazy from the good food and the heat to do more than glare them into slowing down.

Exiting onto South Street, she took the right on Fredonia leading past the elementary school, and another right to go down Cottonwood Street. The old-growth magnolia trees had shed the spring's plate-sized, creamy white flowers. The leaves, big as a man's forearm, normally a shiny dark green, were shrouded in a layer of dust from the hot, dry summer.

The guy at the paint store had it right. There was Old Betsy, with a shiny new trimming of duct tape framing her plastic wrap-covered back window.

Parking the cruiser behind the truck, she ignored the crumbling concrete steps leading upwards and climbed the four-foot bank instead.

Scraps of old, dried paint littered the ground, and, with the mottled appearance of the wood siding the house showed it had been scraped recently. A bright red cooler sat on the front porch, a sure sign workmen were around somewhere.

Flak walked around the side of the house and found Curt engrossed in a halting conversation with a short, dark-haired gentleman also dressed in painter's whites.

Curt said, "After you raspar las pa-ray-days, peen-tay las par-ray-days with the blanca exterior peen-tay, sí?"

"Sí. Raspar de las paredes y pinte las paredes con la pintura exterior blanca." The smaller man, with a persistent smile, added actions to the words, and patted the scraper, the wall, a can of paint, and then the wall again as he spoke. His fluid speech contrasted sharply with the redneck inflections of Curt's struggle with Spanish. He went on. "Hola, Señora Sheriff Anders. Como esta?"

"Muy bien, Jesus."

Curt looked over his shoulder. "Oh, hey, Flak. I'll be right with you." Without waiting for an answer, Curt turned and completed his instructions.

"Then you peen-tay la poo-air-tuh with the blon-ko ez-malt-ay, sí?"

"Sí. Pinte la puerta con el esmalte blanco." The painter walked over to the door, patted it, and then patted the can labeled "Enamel." "Sí?"

"Sí. Gracias, Jesus."

"De nada, señor."

Curt walked over to Flak. "I didn't know you habla'd Español," she said.

"Sí." He held his paint-stained left index finger and thumb about an inch apart. "Poco."

"No," said the other man, who cleaned his scraper as he spoke. "Muy, muy poco!"

"All right, Jesus," Curt turned to Flak again, laughing. "Very, very little. But we get it done one way or another. What's going on with you?"

"Can we sit down and talk a minute?"

"Sure, I could use a drink, anyway. Jesus—you want a Dr Pepper?"

"Gracias, no, señor."

Curt led the way around the house through the weeds and paint chips. He sat near a square post and pushed the entire length of his back along it with a sigh. He pulled the cooler to him and grabbed a bottle of Dr Pepper. "You want one?"

"No, thanks."

"You sure?"

"I'm sure."

"You don't know what you're missing."

Flak watched him take long, luxurious swallows, taking in nearly half the bottle. Pulling the cooler closer, he rested one elbow on it, looking completely comfortable and at ease, with one leg on the ground, and the other stretched in front of him.

She took a seat against the post on the other side of the steps and looked around. The sharp scent of the fresh paint battled with the clean sweat smell of the man in front of her.

"Did you know Dr Pepper was created in Waco and was on the market before either Coke or Pepsi?" He looked at the bottle and then rolled it across his forehead.

"Can't say as I did."

"Yeah, it was named after a real doctor, too."

"Fascinating."

Curt let out a long, rumbling belch and patted his flat stomach. She'd known better than to interrupt his ritual before then.

He started first. "Now, what was it you wanted to talk to me about?"

"I've put a warrant out for your brother's arrest."

"Oh? Which one?"

"Frederick."

He snapped his fingers. "I was hoping it was Ben. Why Frederick?"

Flak chose her words carefully. "I've gotten enough information to believe he might be involved in Tucker's death."

"And what information is that?"

"He had access to the materials that caused the explosion you heard."

"I figured it was the butane."

She shook her head. "Well, you figured wrong. It was turned off at the tank."

"So you just came out here to tell me I'm stupid?" Curt's relaxed tone didn't match the sharp words, as he leaned forward, his elbows on his thighs.

"No. I came out here to talk to you about Tucker and Frederick's relationship."

"I already told you what I knew. Why don't you go talk to his lovely," Curt paused for a less resonant belch, "wife?"

"I'm working up to it."

He said, "Well, I think you're barking up the wrong tree."

"What tree should I be barking up?"

He leaned back against the post once more, with a relieved sigh. "Oh, I don't have any better candidates. You know I'd rat Ben out in a minute, if I thought he'd done it."

"I figured as much, yes."

Curt took small sips from his soda, and outwaited Flak.

"So, has Frederick ever done anything violent around you?"

"He broke my leg, playing football."

"I mean since you've been grown."

"No—but I don't hang around much with the folks he calls friends. I believe in God, but holy rollers make me twitch."

Flak considered her options, and decided she had nothing to lose.

"Look, Curt. I don't really care what your reaction is to Frederick's church members. I need to understand what's driving him right now. He's disappeared. Raylene thinks he's at work. Garrison Oil says he's not expected at work until the first of September."

Most unexpectedly, Curt grinned at her. "Do you remember the Caddy Raylene and Frederick drove up in Saturday?"

Flak nodded.

"Did you notice she had huge, honking diamonds on both hands?" Flak brought up the picture in her mind's eye of Raylene standing behind Frederick, hands on his shoulders, and nodded again.

"Each one is his apology for going off with some chippie."

"Oh, come on! The preacher man fools around on his wife?"

"Yep. Told me once when he was drunk."

"He drinks?" Flak was astounded.

"Only for a month at a time."

"So you're telling me those are all his guilt trips shining off her hands?" She was still having a hard time believing it.

"Yep – furs for winter affairs, diamonds for summer. The Cadillac was for one that lasted nearly a year. He told Raylene he'd been called in a lot that year, too."

"Does Raylene know?"

Curt shrugged. "Never asked her."

"Does anybody else in the family know?"

"Ben, maybe. He's been around for some of those drunks, too."

She questioned him, "So you're telling me Frederick may not be hiding, he may be out screwing around?"

"I'm saying he's probably shacked up with his newest whore, yes."

Flak stood up. She had to know one more thing before she left, though. "Since we're talking about family secrets—do you know if Tucker abused the girls?"

"He abused all of us, sugar."

"I know he tried to kill you, but did he try to molest you first?" Flak couldn't keep the skepticism out of her voice.

"No." Curt's eyes narrowed.

From his reaction, she knew he wasn't going to take her next question well. "I think from some of the things Maggie said, he may have molested her and Jenny. Did you know about it?"

"Maggie says a lot of things." His voice came straight from a blast chiller.

"Do you know anything about it?"

Curt rose, suddenly towering over her with the added height of the porch. "This conversation's over."

"Curtis Lee, just answer the question. Do you know whether or not Tucker sexually abused your sisters?"

The blood rose under his already sun-darkened skin, and his normally sleepy eyes bulged from their sockets. His response started softly. "Not you, not Maggie, nobody will ever make me believe Mama would have asked me to take care of a rapist. She didn't believe it, and neither do I."

"Did Miz Emlyn tell you that?"

"I gotta go back to work." Off the porch in one step, he strode away. Flak watched, as halfway past the side of the building, he wound up the Dr Pepper bottle like a football and threw it violently the length of the back yard. She hoped Jesus wasn't in firing range. Curt never broke stride, never looked behind him, and disappeared behind the house.

Flak retreated to her car. Puzzling the new information around in her head, she took the turns back to South Street automatically. At her office, the fax from Tom Kovax was sitting in her chair. She read through the three attached pages. The first was a list of names and addresses for Curt's four brothers and sisters in his familiar handwriting.

One paragraph caught at her attention.

"I know he beat up on y'all over the years. He's done it to me too—for a lot longer. I know he hurt Mama, too. She let it go a long time ago, and got on with her life. I suggest you do the same. I don't mind taking care of him, but I need money to do it."

One piece of the puzzle clicked into place. She needed confirmation, though. She scrambled around for the bit of paper on which she'd written it and dialed the number for the house next to the Looneyville store.

"Hey, Maggie, it's um… Anita. Can I ask you a couple of questions?"

"Sure. Jenny's over in the store putting final touches on a few things."

"I got the fax from Tom—did Frederick know Jenny lived with you before Curt sent this letter to everybody?"

"Probably not. That was the other thing that ticked me off. Curt called me for the addresses, and I thought he was going to send something to everyone." She snorted in disgust. "Little did I know it was a time bomb."

"You may be closer than you know," Flak muttered. Louder, "So how come you guys get along so well now?"

Flak could almost hear the shrug down the phone. "The same way our family always does. We just don't talk about it."

"One last question."

"Fire away," came the cheerful answer.

"Did Miz Emlyn know what Tucker was doing to you and Jenny?"

"I don't know what you mean." Maggie's voice was suddenly dead flat.

Flak sighed. "I think you do, Maggie." She chose her next words with care. "I think Tucker hurt you and Jenny in ways he never hurt the boys. Did you ever tell your mother he molested you?"

She knew it was a when-did-you-stop-beating-your-wife kind of question, but nothing else explained Maggie and Jenny's undying hatred of the man.

Maggie's words came out slowly, like an old 78 record played at 45 speed. "No. And then yes. Didn't tell her about it when it happened, but afterward. We talked it over a lot—it was part of the healing process for me, and probably for her, too."

"So she knew about it."

The voice on the other end came back to something resembling normal. Maggie said, "I just told you—yes, she knew. Absolutely."

"Then why does Curt think she didn't believe you and Jen were molested?"

Maggie's answer was slow once more, as if she had to make sure each word fit with the others.

"Mama…had a gift for helping us deal with things. When I found out I'd never have children, I called her. She said, 'When you get to the end of the road, you turn.' It may not sound like much, but it was what I needed to hear at the time. Maybe… maybe she found a way to tell Curtis Lee what he needed to hear at the time."

CHAPTER TWENTY-FOUR

Jenny

I was in the kitchen when it started. Hiding and sneaking around to get out of work was my specialty. That day had been pretty much like all the rest—stressful, full of drudgery and hard work. The only peace to be found was in excusing myself quietly and going in the house to make a snack or pinch at something Mama had prepared in advance of our next meal. But that day was different.

Some say in stressful situations time seems to move in slow motion. Not for me. I heard the talking, then the shouting, then the familiar sound of rage. I went back out the back door and stood at what felt like a relatively safe distance. This time, though, he would sling out a question, and my sister actually answered it with words as angry as his. Not just answers, but truthful answers, answers worth dying for. Something obscene about our "happy family."

When he slammed my sister down in the seat at the worktable and reached for the shotgun that was always near, I found myself beside the steps—I wanted to go help her, but I couldn't. I was frozen, watching the muscles in his arms tighten and relax, tighten and relax. His voice was the only one for a long time, and then he fell silent. Then Mama asked him something—I don't know what it was, but his answer was quiet.

I don't remember running into the house. At least, I was trying hard to run, but I felt like he was right behind me, and I couldn't get up enough speed. I busted out the front screen door, and my ten-speed bicycle was right there, leaned on the front porch. I expected to hear the shotgun behind me, but it still hadn't gone off. Frightened is just too tame a word for that incredible panic.

I grabbed the bike, jumped on, and drove it hard up the hill to the road in front of the house. That Texas red clay seemed to drag at my wheels, but somehow being on the bike meant I had some hope. I didn't look back, not even when I heard the engine noise of the truck above my banging heart. He caught up with me about two miles from the house, and used the truck to force me off the road. I piled up in the ditch by the old water tower, but I never missed a beat, just rolled off the bike and got up running.

I knew Miz Anderson's horse, Rusty, was pastured there, just on the other side of the fence around the water tower. I went up the fence, determined to get to him, and as my upper body got over the barbed wire, I felt his hand on my neck, dragging me back. My upper arm ripped on the sharp wire, and I don't remember my feet touching the ground on the way back to the truck. He opened the passenger side door and threw me in. I landed on the shotgun, and sat on it all the way back to the house.

He did not speak, or if he did, I don't remember.

Sitting there on that gun, a sudden peace came over me. My breathing calmed, and my heartbeat slowed. I thought, "We don't have to do this anymore, it's all over. They're both dead, and I'm next."

We got out of the truck together, and he grabbed the shotgun before he slammed his door of the truck.

I went into the living room ahead of him. My sister and my mother sat there, both on the couch. I had expected to see their blood-soaked bodies lying on the ground outside, so their presence was devastating. I thought they would be mad at me because I left. I thought I'd made it worse.

When he came in the door behind me with the gun, we were all sitting there, heads down, waiting for the next move. He looked at all of us, and then he disassembled the gun. He took the pieces outside, and as we watched through the windows, he threw each piece in a different direction into the overgrown pastures near the house.

I don't remember another word said all day. The next day, my sister was gone—to town, he said. Living with Grandpa, he said. I just knew she was gone. Then it all started again—every morning Mama and Daddy fought. All day, because he took us both to work with him on his construction jobs, it was this incredible tension—snapped orders, bland obedience. Unless somebody else was around, then he was all smiles and Texas good-old-boy line of bull.

Watching him put on that act, that's what finally pushed me over some edge I didn't even know existed. When he started pulling his crap at home, I started getting crazy back. And not just a little crazy—suicidal crazy.

The usual dinner-time wrangle was going on—he had decided after my sister left my mother was trying to poison him with her cooking again, so he made me cook for him. He was sitting there sniffing the French fries to see if I'd put arsenic in them, and then he asked me if I thought he was crazy enough to eat it.

I stood up, leaned over the table at him, with both fists down in front of me—I could see Mama out of the corner of my eye, her face almost never held emotion anymore, but she looked scared right then.

I said, "I'm crazier than you old man. And you might want to remember that when you're trying to go to sleep tonight." And I walked out of the room. He avoided me for a while after that.

Mama started in the next day on driving him crazy. He had always gotten complete obedience out of her, and she started defying him in little ways. Just enough to push his buttons all the time. Not enough to get her or me hit, just constant. He finally kicked us out in August on my birthday.

At fifteen, I thought I was finally going to learn how to breathe.

But Mama had her first heart attack the day after we left.

CHAPTER TWENTY-FIVE

Flak looked at the house in front of her car and realized she'd made it from her office to home with her mind completely on automatic. She couldn't remember a single detail of the trip.

Tucker Barnes' death and the actions his family had taken since consumed her every spare thought. No one seemed to have seen or heard from Frederick. Texas was an awful big state to search for one man, particularly when you didn't know what he was driving.

"Crap," she said as she walked in the back door. She meant to ask Curt or Maggie, but had been too wrapped up in the drama with the letter and Frederick's affairs to remember that particular question.

Andy wove a figure eight around her Justin boots, sprinkling cat hair like fairy dust. She bent and picked him up. He butted his head against her chin, purring madly, eyes closed.

"Hey buddy boy—was it a tough day? Did you not get enough nap time?" In answer, Andy squirmed out of her arms, hit the floor, and jumped onto the counter. Sitting next to his empty food dish, he glared at her.

"Oh, so that was just cupboard love, was it?" She got his food down and refilled the dish. She could put it on the floor now, with Barney not around to get in it, but it just didn't seem worth it.

She scratched absently behind Andy's ears, and got a kitty growl in return.

She changed into sweats and was tying her tennis shoes when she heard the car in the drive. Moving the bedroom curtain a quarter inch, she saw it was Garvey.

Back in the kitchen, she pulled paper plates out and stainless steel silverware. The convenience of plastic forks wasn't convenient when you ended up picking bits of them out of your food.

When Garvey knocked on the back door, she yelled at him to come in. He laughed when he caught sight of her at the table, knife in one hand, fork in the other.

"Well, I'm glad I remembered to bring dinner with me—you look a little hungry."

"Bring it on over here, man. I'm starving."

Garvey chuckled as he unloaded white boxes with Chinese characters in red on the sides.

"You want chopsticks?" He pulled two pair in red paper sheaths from the bag.

"Nope," Flak said. "Too slow."

"Well, dig in, girl, don't wait on me. I gotta go see a man about a horse." Garvey headed toward the bathroom, with Andy kitty-catting his every step.

By the time the pair came back, Flak had both plates loaded to the groaning point.

"You could have started without me." He slid a pair of chopsticks out of their paper as Flak forked in her first bite of orange chicken.

She shook her head, her mouth too full to formulate words. After she swallowed, "My mama raised me better than that."

"You know, you never say much about you mama. Or your daddy, for that matter." He leaned toward her, his hand stretched out. She ducked away before she could control the reaction.

"Just getting some fried rice off your chin, girl."

She moved back to her original position and let him remove the food particle—his fingertips were warm on her skin.

He wiped off the rice on the paper towel napkin she'd placed near his place. "Seriously, you don't talk about them much."

"You're right, I don't. You want some tea?"

"Sure." Flak felt his gaze like a weight as she moved past him toward the fridge. She poured them both a glass of tea and made a mental note to pick up plastic cups.

She put Garvey's tea next to him as she walked past.

"Am I over some kind of limit? I'll back up if you want me to."

Flak looked at her food. It had looked really good a few moments before.

"I figured Mary would have told you anyway. It's no big deal."

Garvey shook his head. "She was good at keeping secrets."

Flak shrugged, wondering why it was so hard to say this still—it had been twenty years.

"No secret, really. My dad was a cop in Dallas. He died when I was ten. My little sister was seven. My mom lives with her now up in Princeton. My sister gave her three grandkids and a nice son-in-law. I gave her a redneck son-in-law who she was none too fond of, and no grandkids. I'm not what she wanted me to be. We don't talk much."

Flak took another bite of the food but it had no taste.

She was still staring down at the plate full of food, seeing something completely different in her mind, when Garvey's voice cut through the fog. "What did she want you to be?"

"Anything but a cop."

"Why?"

Flak pushed her plate to the side, put both elbows on the table. "She hated Daddy for getting killed and leaving her with two kids to raise. She said she'd rather shoot me herself than wait around for some criminal to do it."

"Not exactly maternal, huh?"

"It could have been worse. After hearing what Tucker put his girls through, I realized Mama wasn't that bad."

Garvey nodded. "Always somebody worse off than you, kid. Ain't you gonna eat that?" He pointed at her plate. "Thought you were hungry."

"Lost my appetite." Flak patted one thigh absently. "It won't kill me to miss a few bites."

"I never did figure out why women want to be skin and bones. I like them with a little meat on them."

"That right there was one big reason why Mary adored you." Flak laughed. "She was always trying to lose weight."

Garvey nodded, smiling. "I liked her the way she was." He finished the last morsel on his plate and took a sip of tea.

Raising a questioning eyebrow at Flak, he said, "Outside? Smoke?"

"Well you sure ain't lighting that thing up in here."

Flak led the way to the patio table under the trees. Garvey's pipe lighting ritual was comforting in a way she refused to define.

As the smoke drifted aimlessly past her in the light evening breeze, she took an appreciative breath. She gave Garv a hard time about it, but loved the smell once it was lit.

"You still using Captain's Black tobacco?"

"Yep. You like it?"

"Yeah. It smells good out here."

"But not in the house."

"You know it makes Andy sneeze." Flak grinned while she said it. She knew Garvey's opinion of Andy.

"Yep, that was worrying me. Your cat's smoke allergy was right up at the top of my list."

She asked without thinking first, "What is at the top of your worry list, Garv?"

A pause, and then, "You."

"No need to worry. I'm fine."

"Yes, you are indeed fine. But that's beside the point."

Flak chuckled. She kept her eyes closed. Her entire body was relaxed; head leaned on the back of her chair.

It seemed like it was the right time to go ahead and sink into whatever was building between her and the fire chief. "You flirting with me, Ignatius?"

His voice deepened. "You letting me flirt with you, Anita?"

"Works for me, bub."

Her eyes still closed, she floated in the undemanding darkness, aware she had opened a door, and tired of being alone behind it. She was smiling when his lips touched hers.

The distant tinkle of glass breaking pushed an entire set of equations together in head. The solution was so obvious it made her gasp.

Garvey must have misinterpreted the intake of breath. He put one long arm behind her waist and lifted her to her feet, still kissing her.

"No. Get down!" She pushed at his chest.

He didn't move; he was too deep to hear the words. She hooked her leg behind his knee and yanked, then rode his body to the ground as he fell backwards. She looked up as her quiet little house somehow bulged with the explosion—and then there was only darkness.

The next sensation was pain. Wow, what a headache. She put her hand to her forehead, opened her eyes, and narrowed them against the glare.

"What in blue blazes is going on?"

"Hey, girl. You really there this time?" Garv's voice seemed tinny, far away, like her head was under water.

"Garvey? What are you talking about?"

His voice still didn't sound right. "You have a concussion, Flak. A bad one. That's why your head hurts. Yes, I know it hurts. You told me every time you woke up."

"Woke up?"

"You don't remember waking up before because you got hit on the head. Doc says short-term memory loss is normal. And hopefully temporary."

"Garvey?"

"Yeah?"

"How did I get concussed?"

"We'll talk about that later. I have to ask you a couple questions, okay? What day is this?"

"Friday. It's Friday."

"Nope, it's Sunday. Who's the president?"

"Dubya."

"One right. Last time you said Ronald Reagan. What's my real name?"

"Ignatius Royal Garvey."

"Dang. I was hoping that was one thing you wouldn't remember." He smiled at her.

"Sunday? Really?"

Flak's vision quit bouncing around and let her focus on Garvey. He sat next to the bed and held her hand. His hand felt rough. Lifting it, she saw stark white gauze.

"What happened to your hand?"

"Got bitten."

"Who bit you?" Please God, she thought, I hope I haven't gone crazy and started biting people.

"Andy."

Flak closed her eyes. "What did you do to him to make him bite you?"

"Thank you very much for that vote of confidence." His smile was all over his voice, and she needed that right now very much. Felt like her brains were bouncing off the insides of her head, and rebounding off the back of her eyeballs.

Garvey continued. "Your cat is alive and well and mean as hell, but he is a little singed around the edges."

"What the hell happened?"

"I'll just have to tell you again in three or four hours."

"Humor me."

Garvey took a deep breath, and started in reciting—she could tell by the way he said it he'd said it a number of times before. She began to really believe the whole concussion story.

"Your house was firebombed. You took a blow to the head from some flying debris, but neither one of us knew it. You started for the house to look for Andy after the explosion, and I wouldn't let you go in. I opened what was left of the door, and he was standing right there. He must have been under something where he was protected. I grabbed him and pitched him in my car, but not before he bit the living crap out of me. As soon as he was safe, you went down like a pole-axed steer."

Flak opened her eyes, looked at him; yep, he looked a little singed around the edges himself. "Firebombed. Who?"

"Jim says preliminary indications are the same as Tucker's house. He won't be able to confirm for a week or two. I'd place a bet whoever did this was probably the same as the person who shot at you and killed your dog."

"Sounds like a bad country western song." Flak reached past her forehead. Sure enough, just above the hairline was a huge knot, with a big fat bandage over it. She "ouched," and quit playing with it.

She squinted at Garvey. "Any chance you kept it out of the paper?"

He shook his head. "Nope. Even made the Dallas Morning News."

"Crap."

He shot her an amused look. "Maybe you are back with us. I was afraid you were going to have scrambled eggs for brains, girl."

"No," she reached up to gingerly touch the massive lump. "But they ain't exactly sunny side up yet. I feel like I been hit in the head with a two-by-four."

"They didn't want to give you any pain reliever because of the injury to your head. You want me to go check and see if they can now?"

Flak nodded and regretted it. Felt like her brain bounced off the insides of her skull with every movement.

"Be right back." He let go of her hand and was at the doorway in two long strides.

When the door opened again, she said, "That was quick," and opened her eyes to see Curt standing at the foot of her bed.

"You look like shit, Neets."

"That's funny, because I feel like crap. What are you doing here?" She closed her eyes.

"Well, you know I'm still your husband."

"Not for long, I hear tell."

"They had to have somebody sign for you in case they needed to open you up. Garvey told them to call me."

"Ah." Flak nodded again. She just had to stop doing that before her head fell right off her shoulders and rolled around on the floor. The next thought made her sit straight up in bed, to the devil with the pain. "Oh my God. If this made the Dallas news, my mother's going to have a fit and fall in it."

"I called her. Lied through my teeth, told her you were fine."

"And that was a lie because…"

"Because you weren't fine. You nearly got killed, you idiot."

She looked at him, thought about getting pissed, decided against it. Wished she knew for certain sure it wasn't him who had blown up her house, but didn't figure it would be a good thing to say right this second. "Thanks for calling my mom."

"Least I could do."

Silence descended. He still stood there, arms folded, like he was waiting for something. She subsided back against the pillows.

Their last meeting came to mind, and she figured she owed him something for that, as well as soothing her mother's fears. "I'm sorry I got up your nose yesterday about Tucker."

"Wasn't yesterday. It was three days ago."

"Whatever." She waved the time thing away for the moment. "I'm still sorry."

"In the ten years I've known you, I don't believe I've ever heard you say that before."

Flak thought about that. "Maybe the explosion did scramble my brains like an egg."

"Maybe Sheriff Flak Anders has a softer side."

"Nah," they said together after a few seconds. They were still grinning at each other when Garv walked in with the doctor.

If it hadn't been for the moustache, the white-coated stethoscope toter would have looked about twelve years old. Embroidered above the pocket of his white lab coat was P. Karabaggian in blue thread. Made her dizzy to try to read the cursive writing.

He asked Flak to watch his penlight as he moved it around in shiny arcs in front of her face. Her eyes felt like red hot marbles rotating in their sockets.

"I will order some pain reliever for you," he said in a thick accent. "But it will be mild. You gave us a big scare, young lady." He patted her on the arm while she stared at him in disbelief.

Nobody had called her "young lady" in a long time. "We will also watch you for one more night or possibly two."

"No," Flak said. "I want to go home."

Curt and Garv had watched the eye test, arms folded, silent, but this was too much for them. Both started to talk at once. The doctor held up a hand and they subsided.

"If the newspaper I read this morning was correct, while you may still have a home, you will find you do not actually have a house."

"Crap."

"Succinctly and most admirably phrased. And, I must tell you that you must do that, as well, before you are discharged. Plumbing must be in order prior to release. Ah ha. It's a good joke."

"Glad you think so."

"Nurse will pull catheter immediately, but you must be escorted to toilet. No falling down on the job, please." He cackled.

She refused to give him a smile in return—she was still pissed about not being able to go home. "Nurse will bring pain reliever, too. Your gentlemen callers will leave. You will rest, yes?"

She started to nod, stopped herself. "Yes."

"Good." He herded Garv and Curt out the door like a Chihuahua chivvying a pair of longhorns.

Flak sat back with a sigh and touched the lump on her head one more time.

"Ouch."

CHAPTER TWENTY-SIX

Jenny

The twenty-two years after Mama left him were probably the best of her life. I got closer and closer to her as time went by. I guess that's part of why her death was so hard. I couldn't prepare myself, even if I had wanted to, which I didn't. At some level, I'm not sure I believed she would ever leave us.

That heart attack the day after he left was the first, but not the worst. But none of them stopped her. Nothing stopped her anymore.

It was like all her years of silence while she was married to him gave her this huge storehouse of words. She loved to talk. She would still be talking when you drove out of the yard to go home. It was wonderful. She got close to her family again, her mother and her sister.

And we all gathered around her, like chilly people warming their hands over a fire. One holiday, there were so many people packed into her little house, there wasn't any floor space left to take a blanket and curl up. All she asked was that nobody sleep in front of the coffee maker. There were people in the hall, people on every piece of furniture. It was just important to all of us that we be there, with her, as much as we could.

My sister compares us to a bunch of three-legged tables. We do okay as long as you don't put pressure on the corner where the leg is missing.

It was a pretty accurate description of me. My supporting legs were Mama, my sister, and my husband. My father should have been the fourth leg, but I had pretty much removed him from my life. When Mama died, my two-legged table just collapsed. There was no way for me to stay upright. Then when my husband couldn't handle it and left with my kids, I was left with only one support, my sister.

I survived like that for a while, and then the letter came from my brother. This is the only human being who shared the same mother and father as me and my sister. He says we owe him money for supporting the old man.

It was funny in a tragic sort of way, and it was devastating, too. It was like all this work I'd done to get the old man out of my life, to quit thinking about what he'd done, was all useless. My own brother brought that shadow back into my life.

And I gave up again. I had only taken a few of the pills when Maggie walked in. She made me throw up, walked me around the room, the house, the yard, the block.

Basically, she told me it was okay to be angry. That he was wrong for asking, that Daddy was wrong for hurting me and her. So I started getting mad. And I started feeling better. I started feeling a lot of other emotions, too. Some, I hadn't felt in a long time.

Look, whatever this whole wild life has left us with, my sister and I have the capacity to recognize joy. Sound stupid? How many people do you know that have everything they need and want, but still aren't happy?

Any time I start feeling like that, I just turn on a water faucet. Hot and cold running water is a blessing, baby, when you've had to yank every drop of water you get out of a deep well using a steel bucket on an icy rope. That's reality.

Living like we did means you recognize joy when you see it, and you hold on to it and squeeze it for all it's worth. That's something, anyway.

It's one thing.

CHAPTER TWENTY-SEVEN

Flak woke from a dream of fire. A woman stood at the end of the bed. Her many-ringed hands clutched the metal footboard; diamonds glinted in the dimly lit room.

Flak glanced at the window. Night—she must have been out for hours. She could see Garvey's familiar shape in the chair under the window.

She turned her attention back to the woman, who had yet to say a word.

"Hello, Raylene."

"Sheriff." The woman nodded at Flak. "I hear you're looking for my husband."

"Yes." Flak closed her eyes.

"What can I do to help?"

Flak's eyes flew open in surprise. She had braced herself for a completely different response.

"We need to know what he's driving. I was going to talk to you Saturday, but…" Flak gestured to her bed and surroundings. "I kind of got interrupted."

No answering sparkle of humor lit the woman's eyes. She simply stared.

Flak began to feel self-conscious under the scrutiny. "Did you want something else?" The discomfort magnified the headache, and she could feel her own heart beat in rhythm with the throbbing pain just behind her eyes.

"I just wanted to say I was sorry. About your house." Raylene softened her abrupt tone. "I drove by there and it looked like it had drawn the wrath of the Lord upon it."

"I… was not inside when it exploded." Flak hadn't known she remembered that much until she said it out loud.

Garvey stood, startling Flak. "I believe you can give the information on your husband's vehicle to the deputy at the door, ma'am. If you'd be so kind…" He loomed over the woman, who continued to stare at Flak.

It seemed like a long time, but was probably only a few moments before she turned and allowed the big man to shepherd her out of the room without protest.

Flak poked and prodded at the memory she'd gained, but it was like a single stalk of wheat in a field of stubble.

Garvey came back looking thoughtful. "Hey, girl. So the doc was right—you are getting some of it back."

She nodded, and realized it didn't hurt quite as much as it had before. "I guess so."

"Do you remember what we were doing just before the blast?"

Flak shook her head and regretted it.

"That's okay. I do." He sat back in the chair with a sigh.

His words to Raylene replayed in her head, and she had to ask. "What deputy?"

"Excuse me?"

"Why's there a deputy outside the door?"

"Because somebody tried to kill you."

Flak carefully refrained from shaking her head again. "No—somebody tried to kill my house. Apparently, they succeeded."

"Yeah. So?"

"There is one other thing I remember."

Garv appeared in the circle of light near the bed and took her hand in both of his. "What's that?"

"That I knew—that I had it all figured out. It all fell into place. I remember… being surprised at how it all fit together."

"So who do you think is doing all this?"

"That, I'm sorry to say, hasn't come back yet. It's like a word on the tip of your tongue." Flak reached directly in front of her with her free hand, grasping at empty air. "I can almost touch it."

"It'll come back, girl." Garvey soothed her as if she were a child. "It'll all come back."

"I hope you're right."

"Why don't you try to go back to sleep."

"Yeah. Think I will. You staying, Garv?" Flak's eyes were already closed, but she heard him retreat to his chair. She wasn't sure, but just before she dropped off to sleep, she could have sworn he said, "For as long as you'll have me."

The next morning, Flak was dressed and sitting in the chair looking out the window when Dr. Karabaggian walked in, Garv right behind him.

"Your tall friend tells me you are quite impatient to depart our most lovely premises, young lady."

"Yes, sir, I am."

"No more pain?"

"None."

"No dizziness, vomiting, all plumbing works?"

"Yes, sir."

"Then I give you leave to go. Paperwork at nurses' station."

He whirled and was gone. Flak looked at Garv, who was grinning at her like some big ape.

"I just realized I have no earthly idea how I got here or how I'm getting home."

Nothing in the world made Flak feel more helpless than not having a car, but Garvey's next words helped some on that score.

"One of the deputies dropped off your cruiser and a new set of keys for it at my house this morning. And I'm sorry, darlin', but Raylene was right—your house is a goner. What the explosion didn't destroy, the fire did. My boys did the best they could, but there ain't nothing left to salvage, really."

Stubbornly, she said, "I want to go home."

Just as stubbornly, "Tough. You're going home with me."

"I'll go to a hotel or something."

"Nope. You won't."

"Damn it, Garvey!" Flak flinched from the sound of her own shout.

"Yep. Thought so. You lied through your teeth to that poor, unsuspecting doctor. I understand completely, and I won't tell him about it as long as you come home with me."

"Blackmail is illegal, you big ratfink."

Garvey shrugged. "It's just reality. So you want me to tell him your head still hurts?"

A woman in pea green scrubs appeared behind him pushing a wheelchair.

Flak restrained the glare, knowing the pain would show on her face. "No. I'll do it your way."

"Good!" Garvey moved out of the way of the nurse. "Nancy—we need to take her down to the back entrance. A couple reporters are waiting around front."

"Sure, Chief."

Safely away from the hospital and unmolested by the media, Flak gave way to her curiosity. "Why all this sudden urge to take care of poor little ol' Flak?"

"Huh. You ain't a poor little old anything. In fact, I'd bet on you in a fight right now, even with that bump on your head."

"Thanks. I think."

"You're welcome. I'm sure."

The little house had gone downhill since Mary's death. The flowers out front were obviously long gone, and the burned-out grass of high Texas summer crackled underfoot.

Inside, the house was clean, but bare. All the little touches of hominess were gone. Flak remembered her last time in the house, the day of Mary's funeral, and swallowed hard.

She had buried herself in her work, and it just seemed Garvey came her way when they got together, or they ate out somewhere. Made her feel bad to realize how lonely he must have been in this place.

Fresh furniture polish and floor wax scented the air. Garvey sniffed the air like an old bloodhound. "Good, Ethel must have come in this morning."

He gently bumped Flak with his elbow. "Go on girl—second room on the right's yours for as long as you need it."

"I remember." She had stayed many times while Mary struggled through her last illness. Garvey was a fireman, then, and his twenty-four-hour shifts were so hard on the husband and wife that Flak had stayed as often as she could. That had been just one more thing she and Curtis fought over, but it had been worth every minute.

She shook off the memories like a dog coming out of the river, and flinched as the movement set her head to throbbing once more.

"Go on," said the deep voice behind her. "It'll be all right."

Laid out on the bed in her room was one of her uniforms in dry cleaners' plastic, a radio, and a gun and belt her deputies must have dug out of the rookies' bin.

"Who did all this?" She pointed at the clothes and equipment.

"Dorrie," was all Garvey had to say as he dropped her hospital bag near the bed.

Flak looked down at her well-worn sweats. "I need a shower."

"Okay—I'll stick around long enough to make sure you don't kill yourself, and then I need to go to the office."

"I need a robe or something, if you've got one."

"Give me a minute."

She sat gingerly on the edge of the bed. Like a wave pounding the shore, it all came crashing down on her at once. No clothes, no house, no dog. It was all gone.

Just as she feared she'd collapse into tears and make a fool of herself, an orange tabby appeared in the door of the bedroom. Andy was in her lap in one bound, head butting against her chin. He looked like someone had given him a haircut with dull scissors and smelled like smoked kitty.

"Hi, baby!"

He "rowred" in return and settled into her lap.

Garv walked in with one of Mary's pretty pink robes over his arm.

"Hey. I see you found each other." Andy sat up and glared at him. "Sorry he still stinks. He hasn't let me get within five feet of him since I got him here."

"That's okay." Flak scratched behind the cat's steadily-flattening ears. "His bark is worse than his bite."

"Well, I can testify to the bite—but he has yet to bark at me."

Flak lifted Andy onto the bed surface and stood. She tried to put her hands in her pockets, but the sweats had none, so she ended up running her hands down both hips instead.

"Look, Garv. I don't know how to thank you. You've done so much."

The big man took the robe he held and draped it around her. His voice started out low and slow.

"I'm sure we'll be able to come up with something. God dang it!" he yelled and shook Andy off the back of his leg.

He looked down at the tabby, and then at her. "One thing you could do is convince that God-blessed cat I'm not a chew toy."

Flak had to sit down on the bed, she was laughing so hard.

Garvey stalked off toward the living room. "Get in the shower."

"Yes, sir!" she said, still chuckling.

Flak took advantage of Garvey's departure after her completed shower to get in uniform and head for work. She felt like an idiot in tennis shoes, and kept reaching for the hat that wasn't there.

At the courthouse/jail complex, she slipped into her office with no one the wiser. Noiseless shoes might have some benefit, after all.

In the middle of her desk was the preliminary report on the fire. A note in Harley's handwriting on the front page read, "Jim says same MO as Barnes arson, but no bullets found."

She read the report without getting any more than she already knew, but treating it as just another crime let her keep it at a distance, impersonal.

She relaxed at her desk and tried to reclaim the memory she'd come up with while Raylene stood at the foot of her hospital bed. She was still staring into space when Harley appeared in the doorway.

"Dang it, Harley—you got rubber soles on those boots? I never hear you coming."

Harley blinked. "Hi, boss. Welcome back. You want a cup of coffee?"

"No. But I'd like to know if y'all got the information from Raylene Miller on her husband's vehicle."

"Yes ma'am. I took care of that one personally, put it out with an updated APB."

"Anything yet?"

"No, ma'am. But it only went out last night."

"Keep tabs on it for me, will you please?"

"Yes ma'am. Um… Sheriff?" Harley looked down at her feet.

"Yeah, Harley?"

"Chief Garvey's a nice guy."

"Uh-huh."

"That's all I wanted to say."

"Harley."

"Yes'm."

"If anybody needs me, I'll be out at Western Warehouse on the Loop."

Harley shook her head. "I must have missed that call."

"No call. I just need to go buy a hat and boots."

CHAPTER TWENTY-EIGHT
Jenny

Watching Mama die was slow torture, one chunk after another out of my heart, out of all our hearts. I was afraid to leave the room, but the waves of grief just pulled me away from her bedside.

I found my sister standing outside the hospital's side door, pounding her fists on the steel railing bordering the portico. It was the first time since we were children I'd heard her scream.

"It's not fair! She's dying and he's still alive. It's not fair!"

When I arrived at the emergency room, Mama was already gone to some another land in her mind. She was muttering and shifting on the gurney, with her hands plucking at the sheets, didn't respond to touch and her eyes never opened. Only one sentence made sense out of all the words I heard her say.

"That's it! It's a tunnel." She said that, and then moved her hands together, as if to pull a pair of curtains apart. After that, nothing else made sense to me. Her body shut down piece by piece after that.

They tried to save her, but they couldn't. The worst—the absolute worst, was when they came in and said we needed to make a decision to take her off the respirator. It was the only time I ever thought that crackpot doctor she thought so much of was worth a tee-diddly. He said we could let her decide.

By turning off the respirator, he said we weren't insuring her death, we were allowing her to choose life. If she did not breathe, and I'm sure he knew from his tests she would not, then it was her choice, not ours.

Every one of us turned to my sister. Here she's younger than everyone else in the room except me, but they all turn to her. I watched her poll my brothers and me with just a look.

She looked at each one of us and saw something. I couldn't even nod—I didn't know if it was the right thing to do. She turned to the doctor and said "Turn it off." I never knew what that cost her. I never asked. I was really, I think, afraid to know.

And then came the deathwatch. Mama's children and grandchildren around her bed, some praying, some just breathing as if they could breathe for her. She lasted for another four hours. That same heart that had been damaged so many years before by hard work and the stress of living with my father kept beating for four hours without her lungs taking a single breath. It was the longest four hours of my life.

I was like a sleepwalker at her funeral. My kids were there—I remember that much, because our grandmother didn't recognize my daughter. While Grandma may have loved us, my father made sure we were not close.

He avoided relatives whenever possible. Maybe he was afraid they'd see the bruises or the concentration camp look in our eyes. Anyway, that's one of the memories I have of the funeral.

Grandma asking who that little girl was climbing all over the church pew.

After her death, there was nothing. I was numb. I really don't remember trying to commit suicide—I just woke up in the cracker factory one day. I was right in the middle of making something stupid out of something idiotic, like a pot holder out of clay or something when I came back to who I was and what was going on.

By the time I convinced them I was rational enough to operate on any kind of "normal" level, my kids were with my husband in California, and that sent me right off another branch of the old nut tree. No mother, no husband, no children.

I went to my sister's house and stayed in the fetal position for like three months. She was great. No pressure—no "take this drug, it will make you feel better." She just let me lick my wounds until I had some chance of seeing what was going on. Plus, she was the only human being in the world I could talk to about everything and she actually knew what I meant. She knew what living with a rural terrorist was like.

She protects me from the outside, but she doesn't protect me on the inside. Whatever I feel, she makes me face up to it. Gently, but she still does. I guess she got her strength from our mother. Mama was really good about doing the same thing. No horse hockey, as she called it, just lay it out.

We all hide too much from each other, and we still do it with the boys. How do you explain something they will never feel? First of all, they're so uncomfortable with it, they can't even talk about it. And I'm finally getting to the point where I don't have to talk about it.

Talk's cheap anyway.

CHAPTER TWENTY-NINE

The week passed slowly, mostly because Flak peeked around every corner before she rounded it. Every time she stopped to do so, seemed like Harley stepped on her heels. The big deputy was never more than ten feet away from her, at best.

Unlike televised cop shows, neither the results from the APB or the chemical tests from the fire had arrived right after the commercial break. By Friday, Flak was glad to see the courthouse in her rearview mirror.

Evenings with Garvey were the only bright spot in her week. He and Andy had come to an agreement for an armed truce. Andy was armed with teeth, but Garvey had taught him a little respect. The tabby now ignored Garvey with the disdain only a cat can muster.

Flak pulled the cruiser into the drive, unfastened the seat belt and laid her head on the steering wheel. She seldom gave in to the moments of weakness, and never at work.

While the lump had receded, the headaches had continued. She could ignore them when she stayed busy enough, but the pain was never far away.

"You okay girl?"

"Yeah, Garv, I'm fine. Just been a long week, that's all. How was your day?"

"Just another day."

He opened the door for her, and she spied Andy, sitting about ten feet down the hallway. Once he had her attention, he turned and headed straight for the food dish.

Garvey laughed. "That cat is so much like my mother-in-law, it's scary."

"How so?"

"She was fond of taking a chunk out of me every now and then, too. And food was never far from her mind, either."

Flak smiled at him. "Andy's been good lately."

"Yeah—after I thumped him on his hard little head a couple of times. Maybe that's what I should have tried with Miz Betty."

"How is she, anyway?"

"Mean as ever."

Flak headed for her room to change clothes. "What's for dinner?"

The shout came down the hall. "How's Jack in the Box sound?"

"Like a heart attack in a sack."

"What?"

She stuck her head in the hallway. "Never mind! I'll think of something."

Flak looked thoughtfully through the jeans and shirts she'd bought and sighed at the thought of all the other things needed doing. Under the circumstances, Western Warehouse had started her a credit account, but everything had to be replaced. Her wallet and checkbooks had burned, as well.

It was just too much to think about right now, she decided. Good thing she lived in a relatively small town. Being the law didn't hurt either—she didn't have to worry too much about getting stopped for no driver's license when she was behind the wheel of the cruiser.

Flak was feeding Andy by the time Garvey walked out to the kitchen. She'd also had time to explore the bachelor bare cabinets and refrigerator. She had let Garv make the decisions all week, and Garvey's decision for dinner was always eating out or having food delivered.

He must have seen her throw her hands in the air and sigh. "Hey, girl, how about we head for the Caraban? They put in a little supper club there. Your brother-in-law's playing there tonight."

She shook her head. "Ben's not my brother-in-law much longer. The divorce papers got to my office today. I signed them and took them up to Judge Radcliff."

"So what happens now?" Garvey leaned one hip against the kitchen counter, arms folded. "I never went through a divorce."

Flak took the same stance, at a conversational distance away. "As it happens, I haven't either, but I did talk to the judge a little while I was up there. He said with no custody and neither one contesting the divorce, he'd put it at the top of his list. By September sometime, it'll be final."

Garvey nodded. "How you feeling about all that?"

She shrugged. She was doing a lot of that these days. "Better than I thought I would. Especially since it looks like one of my soon-to-be-ex-in-laws has me at the top of a hit list."

"You figuring the divorce will settle all that down?"

"Nope." Flak shook her head firmly. "I don't think my divorce has anything to do with getting shot at or blown up. I think somebody wants me to back off investigating Tucker's murder."

Garvey shook his head mournfully. "I don't think they understand who they're messing with."

Flak shrugged again in answer. She wished she felt that sure of herself, though it was awfully good to hear Garv say it out loud. Neither the insecurity nor the pleasure in his opinion were emotions she was used to.

He slapped both hands on his thighs. "Let's go get on the outside of a good steak, girl."

"Lead on, Chief."

Flak hadn't realized how hungry she was until she looked down and half her New York strip was gone. She refrained from looking at Garvey's plate. Watching the blood run out of a rare steak made her gag. Watching people bleed didn't bother her at all, but then again, she didn't have to watch somebody hack a piece off and eat it, either. The thought made her stomach do a slow roll.

"Why do they call them 'New York' strips, anyway?" Flak tried to distract herself from her thoughts with a little small talk. She'd never been good at it.

Garvey looked up from his carnivorous treat. "The same reason they call them French fries and English peas, I reckon. Makes them sound more interesting."

"Peas are never interesting."

"A truer word was never spoke."

She dug back into her steak until she felt a hand fall on her shoulder. She restrained the impulse to stab the back of it with her fork, afraid she'd miss.

"Well, hello, Sheriff-in-law, how's tricks?" She contented herself with shrugging the hand away.

"Hello, Ben. Pull up a seat."

He whispered in her ear. "You sure that long drink of water across the table won't get all bent out of shape?"

"I'm sure. Sit down." She pointed with her fork at the chair to her right.

He walked past it, and around to Garvey. "Ben Campbell," he said, extending his hand to the other man.

"Garvey," was all the chief said in reply, but he did put his fork down long enough to shake hands.

"Would that be Fire Chief Garvey?"

"Yep."

"I've heard a lot about you."

"All good, I hope." Garvey's voice was unheated, but deeper than usual.

Ben couldn't seem to resist his usual sarcasm, even with someone he'd never met. "Oh, I wouldn't say it was all good, but it wasn't all bad."

"That's nice." Flak kept a weather eye on Garvey—the fire chief didn't suffer fools gladly at the best of time, and she knew Ben's snide remarks would get under Garv's skin in a big hurry.

Ben sat down, and waved the waitress over, "Get me a Coors Light, honey. Have to watch my girlish figure, you know." He patted his flat stomach, looking from Flak to Garvey and back again.

"So I hear you're at the top of somebody's list." He lifted an eyebrow at Flak.

"And who did you hear that from?" She wiped her mouth with the napkin in her lap and placed the white cloth on her plate.

Her appetite was a fragile thing these days. She had a sudden flash of pushing another plate away from her at her now-destroyed kitchen table, but dismissed it. The memories of the night of the fire kept coming back at odd moments, but none told her what she really wanted to know.

Ben took a swig from the beer the waitress placed in front of him. "I do still talk to my family, you know. It's just that, as the black sheep, they look on me as a ba-a-a-a-d influence." His startlingly apt imitation of a lamb made Flak grin in spite of herself.

She figured she'd ask questions until she pissed him off, which knowing him, wouldn't take long. "Have you talked to Frederick lately?"

"No. Should I have?"

"You tell me."

"I stay away from Frederick because his wife is generally in the same room with him when he's in East Texas." He lifted the same black cowboy hat he'd worn the last time she saw him. "You see any horns under here?"

Flak shook her head. All she saw was sandy-brown hair that looked like it was steadily losing the battle to stay on his head. It was quite a bit thinner than she remembered it from family Christmases some years back.

"She thinks I'm the devil himself. I think she's nuttier than a fruitcake. It makes so much more sense to stay away."

"Did you know Frederick was having affairs?"

Ben took a long drink of his beer. "Oh yes. The Cadillac Kid. Diamond Jim. Fooling-Around Freddie." Garvey stirred in his chair, and Ben glanced toward him and straightened his act up a bit.

"Yes. I knew about his affairs. When he drinks, he talks too much."

"Not your favorite brother, then?"

"Ah, well, look at my choices."

"Have you seen Maggie and Jenny lately?"

For the first time since he'd sat down, Flak saw Ben's face soften from its perpetual sneer.

"Yep. Went by the store today. They've got it open, lots of customers, and they're both doing fine. It's funny," he mused. "Maggie seems more like Mama every day. And she's apparently decided to finish raising baby sister Jenny."

"Where were you on Friday night?" Flak watched his eyes—it was like watching steel shutters slam over half-open windows.

"San Augustine. Singing. Any more questions?"

"No, that ought to do it."

He pushed the chair back and looked directly at Garvey for the first time since he sat down.

"Good luck to you, Chief. This one," he hitched a thumb toward Flak, "will be a tough nut to crack." He turned and strode away.

"Now what the heck did he mean by that?" Flak couldn't resist asking.

Garvey shook his head, "I haven't got the faintest clue, and frankly, my dear, I really don't give a hoot. You ready to go home?"

"Yeah—how much do I owe?"

He waved her hand away from the bill. "Nothing. My treat."

She sighed, and met his eyes. "You can't keep feeding me forever, Garv."

He grinned at her. "Sure I can."

The drive back to the house was comfortably silent. Flak headed for her room to pull off her boots.

She grabbed the afghan off the bed, one of Mary's creations, and headed for the love seat where she spent most of her evenings. Andy scrambled after the trailing edge of the crocheted blanket, and swarmed into her lap the instant she sat down.

Flak had wiped him down with a fabric softener sheet every night, which had at least made it where you could be in the same room with him without gagging.

Flak used the remote control to move around the channels, finding nothing worth watching. When Garvey sat down in his recliner, she tossed him the remote control and settled in for a low-stress evening of mindless entertainment.

Hours later, she woke, still on the love seat. The police band radio on the end table crackled again, and she realized it had woken her up. She listened to the traffic long enough to realize she must have missed something, and phoned Dorrie.

"Hey girl, what's going on?" she said at the sound of the night dispatcher's voice.

"Oh, just the usual, Sheriff. Jasper Jay's neighbors called, said the fights were on. I sent Harley out there."

"What's Harley doing working night shift?"

"She took on a double for Cliff. His wife's birthday or something like that."

"Okay. Call me at this number if you need me."

After a quick bathroom break, she got back under the blanket and rubbed her air-conditioning-frozen feet on Andy. He batted at her icy toes with his clawless front paws, biting them between swats.

When the phone rang, they both jumped.

"What's up, Dorrie?"

Flak had never actually heard Dorrie sound upset before—the big woman took everything in stride. But her voice was high, hurried and distressed.

"Harley's out there to the Rawlins' place, and she says Jasper Jay's dead."

"I'm on my way."

CHAPTER THIRTY

Jenny

I always thought of funerals as these barbaric rituals, you know? Weird things the living do in order to feel better about not being dead themselves.

But for me, and I think for my brothers and sister too, there was something about all the ceremony and tributes to Mama that helped.

Of course, I fell off my branch of the nut tree a few weeks after, but it wasn't because of the funeral. It was because she was no longer present in the world. I just couldn't get that to reconcile at all, so I went a little whack. Okay, a lot whack.

The funeral was a celebration of her life as well as a mourning of her death, and my father's name was nowhere. It was like we were finally able to erase him from her history. The funeral home was packed, and although a significant number of the attendees were my brothers' ex-wives, that was satisfying, as well.

Watching her sons and grandsons and son-in-law bear her casket to the grave was the worst part. Their faces, all frozen in grief, made me understand what we all looked like. It made it real, somehow. I'd been wandering around in a fog for days, and it seemed like, when the sun broke through, it burned a hole right through my heart. The gaping wound left by her absence never healed. She was and is irreplaceable.

I've tried to join her; I've tried to forget her; I've tried to replace her with my sister's love. None of it worked.

I tried writing letters to her for a while, on the advice of my first shrink. I found myself lying to her in my letters because I didn't want to upset her, so that didn't work either.

My sis told me once losing her was like getting the skin over your entire body rasped off with a cheese grater. As soon as you think you're starting to heal, somebody comes along and pours gasoline over you, and the sores all break open again.

It's kind of like that.

CHAPTER THIRTY-ONE

Flak left a quick note for Garvey, threw on her uniform and headed for the Loop. She was careful not to turn her siren and lights on until she was well away from the house. As she rounded the gentle curves of the highway around the city, she hit speeds over a hundred miles of hour, scaring the usual assortment of drunks and evening shift workers out of their complacency.

She cut the siren before entering the little housing development on Boozer Street, but it made no difference. A dozen folks had gathered, most wearing bathrobes of uncertain vintage, for their biweekly entertainment. This would give them something to talk about for months, Flak was sure.

She nodded to the emergency medical technician in the van, and met the other halfway up the stairs to the front door. "Hey, Grant."

"Sheriff."

Flak kept her voice quiet—no sense giving the gossips any more ammunition than they already had. "What's his status?"

"Dead as a hammer. And he looks like one was used on him. I don't think I've ever seen anything worse, Flak."

"Why don't you and your partner give me a minute, okay?"

"Yeah—he's radioing for Doc Adams now. We need him to declare an official time of death."

"Thanks."

Even with his comment, Flak was unprepared for the scene inside. The normally pristine living room was a shambles—a crazily tilted lampshade cast odd shadows, and the blood on the furniture and the floor faded from red in the light to black in the unlit areas. By accident or design, the harshest glare was cast on Jasper Jay. He lay face up in the middle of the living room rug.

What was left of his face was up, anyway.

Harley stood in the entrance to the tiny kitchen, her ordinarily ruddy complexion a dark gray.

"What happened, Harl?"

"It was my fault. I was late. If I'd only have gotten here sooner… but I was late."

"It's not your fault."

"I forgot it was payday at the plant. I ain't worked night shift in so long. I just clean forgot." Flak could hear in her voice the big deputy was near tears.

"You didn't kill him. Where's Faith-Ann?"

Harley moved out of the doorway. Faith-Ann Rawlins sat at the tiny kitchen table sipping from a cup. Blood spattered her flowered robe, and added unholy freckles to her face and the backs of her hands.

"Why the hell is she still here? And why isn't she in cuffs?" Flak kept her questions quiet.

"She said she'd only go with you. Said you'd know where to take her. She didn't seem too dangerous, so I didn't cuff her yet."

"Has she been read her rights?"

Harley's voice stayed low, as well. "Yes ma'am, but I don't think she was listening."

"Where's the weapon?" She was despairing of getting much from Harley. The big woman was so distraught, she was past being useful at this point.

"I haven't found it yet."

"Look—Doc Adams is on his way. Help him when he gets here. I'll talk to her."

"Yes, ma'am."

Harley edged into the living room, looking everywhere except at the body. Flak took pity on her.

"Go outside and tell all those people to go home."

"Yes, ma'am." The relief in Harley's voice was evident. She placed her size twelves carefully on the way to the door.

Flak did her best to avoid the blood on the way into the kitchen, but it was everywhere.

Faith-Ann seemed to realize she was there for the first time.

"Hello, Sheriff. Would you like a cup of tea?" She started to rise from the chair.

"No. No thank you."

The stocky woman settled back into her chair, took another sip and stared into space with a gentle smile.

"Faith-Ann, do you remember the deputy reading you your rights?"

"Oh yes. Anything I say can and will be used against me in a court of law." The giggle that followed her statement was so unexpected, it left Flak at a loss for words.

"As if I could be judged in the courts of earthly law. Ain't that funny?" She giggled again. "The

Lord God saw fit to use me as his weapon, to punish the wicked through me."

The smile disappeared and Faith-Ann took on a serious look. "God Almighty judged Jasper Jay and found him wanting. I carried out His bidding."

She smiled again, a radiant beam that turned to Flak's face for the first time. No, not to Flak's face, behind her face.

With an effort, the sheriff resisted looking behind her. She knew she'd see nothing except the ruins of a man in a slaughterhouse of a living room.

"And now you're here, as God told me you would be, to take me to the city of refuge wherein his kinfolk cannot revenge themselves on me. I will be safe there. He told me so. Until the anointed priest dies, I will be safe."

"What did you use to carry out that bidding?" The sturdy woman did not respond.

"Faith-Ann!" Flak said sharply, and finally gained the other woman's attention. "What did you use to carry out God's justice?"

Without another word, Faith-Ann reached toward the chair next to her, the seat of which was hidden from view. She pulled out a tire iron covered with blood, and placed it on the table surface in front of her.

Without conscious thought, Flak said, "Oh, my God."

"Yes He is your God, and mine. I am His." Once again Faith-Ann aimed that blinding smile toward Flak.

The officer of the law thought frantically. "May I take it, Faith-Ann? Umm, and preserve it in a holy place?"

"Oh, yes. Here." Faith-Ann rose and handed the gory prize to her. Flak put one finger under the curve to keep from leaving her prints all over it, but had to grasp it fully anyway, to keep from dropping it to the floor. Faith-Ann handled the thing like it was a toothpick, but it was heavy.

"Have a seat, Faith-Ann. I'll be back to take you to the uh... city of refuge." Flak stood stock still a moment. That phrase struck her as so familiar. Where had she heard it before?

She shrugged it off mentally. There had been too many of those flashes in the past week, all useless.

"Just stay right there, Faith-Ann." The woman nodded and took another sip of her tea. She thought for a moment, realized she was doing the same thing Harley had done, leaving her without cuffing her, but didn't see a whole lot of options.

Outside, Flak yelled for Harley, who hurried around the ambulance, already in verbal flood.

"Doc Adams should be here any minute."

"Get an evidence bag out of your trunk for this." Harley visibly paled in the dim light of the streetlights at the sight of what Flak held. "Oh my God, where was that?"

"Right next to Faith-Ann the whole time. Take it as a lesson. Never, ever turn your back on a suspect, you understand me?"

"Yes, ma'am." Harley hung her head.

"Get me an evidence bag."

Flak held the weapon as gingerly as she could until Harley returned with the bag. She carefully placed the wicked looking piece of iron in the bag. "Hang on to that."

"Yes, ma'am."

"I'm going to walk Faith-Ann out here and get her in my car. Keep everybody clear."

Harley nodded.

Flak edged around the bloody mess in the living room once more.

"Faith-Ann, it's time to go."

"Yes. Just let me wash this cup."

"No, leave it. I have to um, keep you safe from those who would seek revenge."

"Yes, of course," Faith-Ann murmured.

The woman walked, oblivious, past the wreckage that had once been a man, once been her husband, and waited patiently as Flak opened the cruiser's back door. Flak shut it with a sigh after getting her settled, and got in the driver's side.

The trip to the jail was at a much slower pace than her wild ride to the scene. Flak radioed ahead and asked Dorrie to have Jerry meet her at the car.

Trying to get a handle on her earlier memory flash, she interrupted Faith-Ann's tuneless humming. "You know the Bible so well—where might I find that passage on cities of refuge?"

"Numbers 35, verse 25. 'And the congregation shall deliver the slayer out of the hand of the revenger of blood, and the congregation shall restore him to the city of his refuge, whither he was fled: and he shall abide in it to the death of the high priest, which was anointed with the holy oil.'"

"Yes, of course," Flak murmured. Faith-Ann went back to herself once more, and the humming began again.

Jerry waited in the parking lot when they arrived. Flak explained carefully it was safe to go with him. "He is the head of the congregation, Faith-Ann. He's here to take you to your place of refuge."

Softly, to Jerry, "Get her a jumpsuit and put all her clothes in an evidence bag." He nodded.

The big jailer walked down the hall holding Faith-Ann's elbow, and Flak collapsed at her desk. She put her head on her folded arms, and allowed the grief to wash over and through her, mixed with a little self-pity for her continuing headache.

Where had she heard that phrase before? It was in a woman's voice—that much she remembered. The fogging throb of pain was like a wall obscuring everything except a few small glimpses.

Flak woke stiff and sore and checked the clock on the wall. She'd slept for nearly an hour—the timepiece said four a.m.

She started poking and prodding at the memory of the phrase "city of refuge." It was almost clear now. "Raylene—oh, my God, it was Raylene who said it!"

She picked up the receiver next to her and started scrabbling the papers around on her desk. Where was the number?

Finding it, she punched it on the phone's dial pad. Maggie picked up on the first ring.

"Hey, it's Anita."

"Hello, how are you?"

"Just peachy—look, I'm sorry to call you this early, but have you seen Raylene lately?"

"Uh-huh."

"Did she say anything to you about 'cities of refuge'?"

"No, I wouldn't say that at all."

"You sound funny—is everything okay?"

"No."

"Is she there?"

"No."

"Is Frederick there?"

"Yes."

And the phone went silent in Flak's hands.

CHAPTER THIRTY-TWO

Jenny

I dreamed of killing him all the time from probably ten or eleven years old until me and Mama left him. And then some. It's funny, you know, because we never talked about it. The brothers and sisters, I mean. Or Mama. Afterwards, we found out we had all thought about it, including Mama.

What's even funnier is he was absolutely paranoid because he thought she was trying to kill him. My sister had to cook for like two years when he decided Mama was trying to poison him. Took her that long to figure out that, if she cooked badly, he'd quit making her do it. And she's supposed to be the smart one in the family.

All my brothers and sisters finally talked about it as a group on the night of Mama's funeral. Every single one of us had a different method in mind— guns, fire, poison, staking him out in the hot sun on an ant bed. Can't remember the other one.

Oh, that's right. He never actually mentioned what he had in mind, just nodded while we were talking. I remember that conversation very well. It was the best distraction from a truly horrible day.

All our various husbands and wives were wandering around—none of our spouses liked each other much—and the five of us sat on Mama's front porch and talked and laughed throughout this amazingly cold-blooded conversation.

Then, like every other gathering ever held at Mama's house, it went downhill from there. I guess it's funny that, as much as we cared about Mama, she was truly the only thing we all had in common. Losing her shattered more than just *my* tentative grip on reality. I think the rest of them wandered around lost for a couple of years, too.

Anyway, the night of the funeral ended up with one grandchild's nasty boyfriend yelling obscenities in the front yard. Another grandchild brought a six pack of beer—which Mama would have probably thought was funny—and several in-laws got all scandalized. The usual family gathering.

It was the last time we were all together in the same place at the same time. Every holiday we'd ever been together, somebody showed their butt. That's a quaint old East Texas phrase meaning someone made an ass out of themselves.

Usually, it was one of the in-laws on that score, too. Mama started a joke where she would award this little trophy she picked for ten cents at a garage sale. It was the south half of a northbound horse, tacked to a wooden pedestal. If she ever really did hand it to anyone, I never knew about it, but she talked about it a lot. We laughed so much when we were there with her. I miss her every day.

Even with all the things she knew my sister and I went through, even with all the years of talking it all out, there was one more thing I needed her to know. But I couldn't break her heart. Her poor, damaged heart that was finally, in the end, the last of her mortal existence, past breath, past life itself.

I couldn't tell her.

CHAPTER THIRTY-THREE

Flak took the curves on Farm-to-Market 343 at speeds that repeatedly came close to disaster. Holding the cruiser on the road took all her attention.

Before she left the office, she'd asked Dorrie to call Cliff and yank him out of his wife's arms. Harley had enough on her plate with Jasper Jay's murder. Flak instructed Dorrie to stay off the radio about whatever situation was boiling up in Looneyville, too. The last thing she needed was for Curt to hear it on the police band and come walking into an already tense situation.

She buried the speedometer needle out of sight on the straightaways, but it just wasn't fast enough. As she headed up the last hill to the T-stop, she turned off the roof lights. She had run the road without her siren. In the still of early morning, it could be heard for miles.

She cut her headlights off at the stop sign, and killed the engine a few yards before the gravel of the parking lot crunched beneath her tires. She drifted under the carport at the store, getting the cruiser out of sight of the trailer.

She drew her gun and moved silently around the side of the store toward the other building. Maggie's was the only car visible, but Frederick had to have gotten there somehow. The tiny little town was five miles from anywhere. The lone streetlamp made her feel like she was under a spotlight, but there wasn't much she could do about it. Every light in the trailer house was blazing, so hopefully it wasn't easy to see outside.

She edged around the curved end of the metal home, and there behind it sat an ancient Chevy truck, the same make and model Raylene had given them for Frederick. If he was still here, maybe the girls were unharmed. She sniffed the air. The old truck was burning oil.

That gave her an idea. She found the hood catch and carefully lifted it. She yanked the sparkplug wires off the distributor cap. Wouldn't permanently disable it, but it might slow him down. She didn't slam the hood, just let it down easy.

Trying to think of everything that could possibly go wrong was giving her a monster headache. She pushed it back as far as she could and concentrated on her next move.

Flak inched up the back stairs to the door that led into the utility room and back hallway. Though the glass was uncovered, there was no angle to view the rest of the house, no reflections available to get a glimpse of what might be happening. She risked turning the knob and was rewarded by slight rotation of the chilled metal under her hand.

She hastily pulled her boots off, and restrained her usual grunt of effort to do so. The boots would give her presence away immediately on the tile floors of the back entrance. Any heavy step in a trailer house could be felt from end to end.

Flak eased the door open a millimeter at a time to avoid the sucking sound of the weather stripping against the metal frame, and, gun first, stepped inside. Just as carefully, she eased the door shut, but stopped it before it could engage completely.

Still no sound, no movement anywhere. The lights were so bright they hurt her eyes, and she knew her next move would make her visible from any direction.

She looked around, discarding one wild solution after another, until her eyes lit on the electrical panel next to the door she'd just come through. It was time to level the playing field. She hoped she wouldn't precipitate a panicked reaction from Frederick, but her tools were limited.

She gently thumbed the latch upward, and flinched at the click she could barely hear as the door swung open. Alert for anyone coming from either direction, she found the largest lever on the board with her fingertips, took a deep, quiet breath, and pushed it upwards. Darkness descended, and with it, voices. Was that Jenny's quickly stifled scream of alarm? Or Maggie's?

A male voice. Frederick? "Sheriff, if that's you, and I'm pretty sure it is, since we heard you pull up, you might want to know I've got a knife at Maggie's neck."

Flak heard a woman clear her throat. "He's telling the truth, Flak." Her tones were flat, almost unrecognizable. "Turn the lights back on."

Flak hesitated.

"Now, Sheriff!" The deeper voice was unmistakable.

Resigned, Flak reached over and flipped the switch back down.

"Get in here where I can see you."

Flak looked at the gun in her hand, decided it was better to know where it was than to hand it over, and tucked it between two folded towels sitting on the dryer.

She padded through the kitchen in her sock feet and into the living room. Her hands were at her sides, spread wide open to show they were empty.

"Far enough." Frederick was behind Maggie from Flak's viewpoint, both sitting on the couch. His right arm draped around her shoulders, a hunting knife with an eight-inch blade gleaming at her neck.

One quick pull and Maggie's jugular would be wide open. The corded muscles standing out on his forearm showed he had strength enough to sever her spine with the murderous weapon.

Jenny sat on the loveseat, out of his reach. Her knees were clenched tight in her circling arms, and her blonde locks were limply damp, with sweat or tears, Flak couldn't tell which. Maggie's face was calm, but her eyes gave the lie to that serenity.

"Where's your gun?" Frederick's face was unreadable, still as that of a poker player. His mouth opened to snap out the questions, but there were no twitches, no tells.

"In my car." She spread her hands wider for his inspection, turned so he could see the empty holster at her side. Thinking fast, "It's policy—never bring a weapon into a hostage situation."

"You're lying."

She shrugged.

"Turn around."

She did so.

"Pull the back of your shirt up where I can see your belt. Slowly."

Flak did so.

"Now pull your pants legs up."

Flak showed him there was no ankle holster. She hadn't had time to buy one since the fire.

"So you did leave it behind. Not too bright."

She shrugged again, and slowly turned around to face the disaster to come. It was nice he thought that. Maybe he'd underestimate her later.

"Who else knows you're here?"

She shook her head. "No one—my deputy's dealing with another case."

He moved the knife away from Maggie's skin long enough to flick her neck with the point. She made a face, but kept her body still. Blood welled and then spilled down her neck, staining the lace of the robe she wore.

"Try again. Who knows you're here?"

Flak gave up on that tack. "A deputy should be headed this way shortly."

"Not much time."

Flak wasn't going to tell him that, if Cliff didn't answer his phone, Frederick had all the time he could use.

"Jenny." While Frederick's attention shifted away from Flak to the younger girl, the knife stayed at Maggie's neck. "It's time to decide. Come with me. Nothing else has to happen. "

"If I go with you, will you let Maggie go?" Jenny lifted her chin from her knees long enough to answer, but stared at Flak, avoiding Frederick's eyes.

His blank, poker face filled with movement and life when he spoke to Jenny. "I swear. The minute we get far away."

"No," Maggie shouted. Without even looking at her, Frederick slid his knife hand past her throat and tightened his arm. Flak knew all he had to do was grab Maggie's forehead and twist, and he'd break her neck, but she hoped he needed the older sister for leverage with Jenny.

Maggie's eyes bulged, and she grabbed at his arm. Maggie's blood smeared along the rock hard length of it, but the arm moved not one whisker, as far as Flak could see.

"Stop!" Jenny's shriek bled into sobs, and she buried her face once again in her knees.

"Okay. Jenny, I'll stop. I'll do anything for you, Jenny. I already have."

Flak stilled her instinctive move to help Maggie with an eye to the knife that was still far too close for comfort. She took a deep breath along with Maggie's first tortured gasp. The trapped woman clutched the arm restraining her movements and sucked in huge gasps of precious air.

"Frederick." Flak spoke softly, between Maggie's tortured breaths. She watched the knife slide once more to threaten the desperate woman's neck. "Every cop in Texas is looking for you already."

He looked only at Jenny. "The state line's only sixty miles away."

"Then all the Louisiana cops will be looking for you, too." Flak dropped her hands behind her back, eased her knees, and took up a parade rest position.

Maggie's breathing finally slowed to something resembling normal, though it was obviously still painful. Her eyes stayed glued to Flak.

"You're already wanted for murder and assault on an officer. Don't make it worse."

The big man's eyes never left Jenny. "Killing Tucker wasn't a crime, it was justice. Just for you, Jenny. Now he can't hurt you anymore."

Frederick leaned toward Jenny, and Maggie went with him, straining to keep her neck off the knife. "Jenny. We can be together. Always. No one will ever hurt you again."

The younger woman clenched herself tighter into her ball, as if the fetal position could protect her and her sister both. Muffled, she said. "I don't believe you."

Frederick returned to his original position, and Maggie swayed with him. The pain on his face was a stark contrast to his earlier stillness. He opened his mouth to say something, but the crunch of tires on gravel interrupted his thought.

Flak realized everyone in the house had known the moment she drove up—there was no other sound like it.

"If that's your man, you better stop him now."

Flak stepped to the window, but the predawn light showed her something she had not expected at all. She stepped back to her earlier footprints in the soft carpet and shook her head. "It's not my deputy."

Maggie's lips moved in a name, and Flak gave her a miniscule nod in return.

The knock on the door made Flak start, even though she was expecting it. Maggie must have jumped too. Either the old cut or a new one bled in another slow streak toward her collarbone.

"Your call, Frederick. You hold all the cards." Flak wasn't sure what was going to happen, but she had to make him believe he was in control as long as it kept Maggie alive.

"Jenny." The younger woman's entire body jerked in response to Frederick's voice. "Get rid of them."

Jenny unfolded. Her ravaged face looked ten years older than the last time Flak had seen her. She cracked the door open, but before she could say anything, the visitor barged past her into the living room, flinging the door wide open.

"Well, I'm glad to see you're up, but you need to get some clothes on. Garage sales start at daylight." Raylene was fishing in her purse for something, but stopped dead, hand still buried, as she took in the frozen scene.

She took a step forward. "Freddie?"

"Stop right there."

"But…"

"Not a word, Raylene. For once in your damn life, shut up!"

Raylene's clamped her lips together.

The big man barked out a command. "Jenny, close the door and sit down." Jenny edged past Raylene and sat once more on the love seat.

Frederick spoke softly to his wife. "I'm sorry. I didn't want you to know like this."

"Know what? Like what?" Raylene's voice was harsh, demanding.

"I'm not coming home."

Raylene smiled. It was the first time Flak had ever seen a genuine smile from the woman. "I could have told you that." Flak blinked. It was not the answer she'd been expecting.

A disappointed look crossed Frederick's face. He had obviously expected a different reaction as well.

Flak reached forward and touched Raylene's arm to discourage her from antagonizing him further, but the other woman shook her hand off and moved a step nearer to the couch.

"Did you the think the Lord would not tell me who you are?"

Frederick's eyes were riveted on Raylene. Flak froze for a moment, undecided, but the knife had not wavered from Maggie's neck.

"The law stands here to judge you." Raylene gestured toward Flak with her left hand. "For this is how it has to be. While they looked for you, I took up the Book and I studied. Long and hard. I was guided to Timothy first. 'The law is not made for a righteous man, but for the lawless and disobedient.'"

She paused. "'For murderers of fathers.'" Her tone took on the cadence of a preacher at a tent revival, and she took another step closer to Frederick.

With each step Raylene took, Flak took one back. Back toward the laundry room, back toward the gun.

"Then the Lord led me to Jeremiah—'Will ye steal, murder and commit adultery?'" Raylene ground down on the last word, and Flak realized she knew about Frederick's indiscretions, she'd probably known for a long time.

"Will you 'swear falsely…and walk after gods whom ye know not?'"

Raylene's voice was hypnotic, mesmerizing and still she stepped closer to the man who couldn't seem to look away. But the knife gleamed in the light, and Flak backed one more step.

"But the old man was your god, wasn't he Freddie?" The woman's voice dropped to the tones of a mother soothing a child. "He was the only father you ever knew. And he was evil walking the earth." Her voice began to rise once more.

"I was led to Matthew then. 'But whoso shall offend these little ones which believe in me, it is better that a millstone were hanged about his neck, and that he were drowned in the depth of the sea.'" Again, the cadence dropped, and Flak took one more aching step backward.

"But East Texas has no seas, and so he burned. You gave him that foretaste of his eternity. His death was a gift to her, I know. But God led me to one other verse."

Flak's step was exquisitely timed with Raylene's. Every muscle trembled.

"He led me to Leviticus. 'And if a man shall take his sister, his father's daughter, or his mother's daughter, and see her nakedness, and she see his nakedness, it is a wicked thing.' A wicked, evil thing, Freddie. 'He shall bear the iniquity.' Do you understand?"

Flak didn't wait for Frederick's response, but dove backwards for her gun. As she did, the shot rang out behind her.

CHAPTER THIRTY-FOUR

Jenny

Let's get this over with.

I went to my brother for comfort once, after my father had hurt me badly. My brother raped me, too.

It broke something inside of me, something my father's beatings and sexual abuse never touched.

That's all I've got to say.

CHAPTER THIRTY-FIVE

Where the hell had the gun come from? Flak waded back into the chaos in the living room, not even sure who shot whom. Maggie was bent to the couch seat, holding her neck. Blood seeped through her fingers. Flak's view of Jenny was obscured by Raylene, who stood paralyzed a few steps from Frederick. The hand that had been in her purse now obscured her mouth. Flak could see the handbag hanging from her shoulder showed the results of firing a gun through leather.

A bloodstain widened on Frederick's chest. He looked down at his reddening shirt, raised a hand to it, and then struggled to rise, hunting knife still in his hand. The big bull of a man didn't know he was dead yet.

"Freeze!" Flak leveled her gun at his head, but Frederick continued to rise. She steadied her right wrist with her left hand. He lurched forward one step, and the knife began to move toward Raylene. Her hand still to her mouth, the woman backed away. Flak put a bullet into Frederick's right ear. Blood and brain matter blew all over the love seat and Jenny from the exit wound.

Frederick's massive body finally took the hint and collapsed like a sack of feed. The smell of cordite and human waste filled the room. His sphincter had loosened in death, the part they don't often mention in criminal justice classes.

The welcome crunch of gravel accompanied by red and blue lights bouncing off every surface signaled the cavalry's late arrival.

Flak checked on Maggie first. "How bad is it? Can you talk?"

Maggie's grateful eyes said everything else, but she stuck to the subject. "Shallow, I think. I'm just bleeding like a stuck pig."

"If you can walk, head outside then—let my deputy take you to the hospital. It would take a half hour to get an ambulance out here." Flak turned to the other woman. "Jenny. Jenny! Are you all right?"

The younger woman uncurled from her defensive position and nodded. Tears streamed down her face.

"Help Maggie. Go with her." Jenny nodded again, and went to her sister, began helping her toward the door.

"Tell Cliff I said to radio ahead and get the coroner out here."

Raylene stood over Frederick's body, both hands to her mouth now, and not a tear to be seen.

"Raylene." No response. "Raylene!"

Flak kept her pistol ready. "Give me the gun. Carefully, please."

The other woman dropped her hands from her mouth. For the first time, Flak noticed they were bare, not a diamond ring in sight.

Raylene reached in her purse and, without ever taking her eyes off Frederick, handed the gun to Flak, who took a deep breath and let it out slow.

"I think you and I need to talk."

* * *

"And she did." Flak left off her story for a moment and saw Garvey push his plate away, like she'd ruined his appetite. It might have been the blood and brains part that got him or maybe the smell afterward. It got to some people that way. Funny, Tucker's burned corpse hadn't seemed to bother him.

Flak finished her own food while Garvey waited, fingers drumming on the table.

"So—what's the end of the story."

"Oh, okay. There was one piece of information we were missing all along. When Tucker raped Jenny, she went to Frederick for comfort. He raped her, too, telling her he loved her the whole time. That's when she really started going off the beam. She held it together as long as their mother was alive, but when Miz Emlyn died, it was more than she could handle. I talked to her and Maggie at the hospital and confirmed all this. Anyway, Maggie never knew. Actually, nobody but Jenny and Frederick knew."

Flak took a drink of her iced tea and put both elbows on the table. It wasn't her little kitchen table at home, but she was starting to like eating dinner with Garvey most nights.

He shook his head. "I still don't understand. How did all this get started?"

"That's the interesting part. This started in March. When Curt sent that letter out to everybody, he included a front sheet with their addresses and telephone numbers. It was the first time in years

Frederick actually knew where Jenny was. He'd stayed in touch with Maggie, but she hadn't told any of the brothers Jenny was living with her until Curt asked for a mailing address for everyone."

"What letter are you talking about?"

"The letter asking for back support for Tucker and for monthly support checks going forward."

"You have to be joking!" Garvey laughed. "He really expected those girls to help feed and care for their daddy, the child molester?"

"No joke. He said he was desperate. It was one of the reasons he stayed a suspect as long as he did."

Garvey leaned back in his chair, then forward again, putting both elbows on the table. "You mean you suspected Curt of killing his own daddy?"

"I suspected all of them. Every stinking one."

Flak picked up her plate and Garvey's and walked in the kitchen. He grabbed the glasses and put dishes in the dishwasher while the conversation continued.

Flak put a plate in the bottom rack and paused. "Now you have to understand some of this is guessing. With Frederick being dead and all, we're never going to know all of it. But I'm pretty sure he set that fire out in Looneyville to get rid of those people that owned the store."

"What possible reason would he have for doing that?"

"Because he knew Maggie pretty well—knew she thrived on challenge. And even more than that, he knew she wouldn't be able to restart the store alone, so he suggested she bring Jenny."

They finished up the dishes and Garvey did the necessary to get the machine started. "Keep going," Garv said as they walked back in the living room. Flak threw herself in her accustomed spot on the couch with a sigh.

"Well, Frederick did set the fire that killed Tucker, which we pretty much knew already. What we didn't know was that Raylene knew about it, too, because he told her. He lied about the reason, though. He told her it was for the way Tucker treated Miz Emlyn, and her.

She kind of choked up on it when we were talking, but evidently the old man made a really nasty pass at Raylene. Frederick knew that, and knew Raylene well enough to know how to make Tucker's death make sense in her biblical view of how the world works."

Flak got up and began pacing around the room.

"The rest of it I put together from what Raylene told me and talking to Maggie and Jenny in the hospital early this morning. After my house got firebombed, Raylene stopped to talk to Maggie and Jenny at the store.

She knew we were after Frederick, and she wanted to sound them out on what they knew. Well, somehow they got on the subject of Tucker and his rape attempts. Jenny said, although not in so many words, that one of the brothers had raped her too— which was news to Maggie and Raylene. Eventually, they got it out of her it was Frederick.

Well, right after that, Raylene showed up in my hospital room and gave us the information on her husband's vehicle. What he'd done to his own sister was more than she could handle in that religious framework of hers. She could cope with the eye-for-an-eye stuff, but not with incest."

Garvey tapped his finger on his lips while she paced. "What about Barney?"

She took a deep breath. "That's actually the hard part." She sat down on the couch once more, elbows on her knees and hands interlaced.

"Raylene's the one who shot Barney, used me for target practice and set the house on fire."

"Excuse me?" Garvey sat forward in his recliner.

Flak made settle-down motions with her hands. "If Raylene's telling the truth, and I'm pretty sure she is, Barney was an accident, but it takes some explaining."

She sat back on the couch and tucked her feet under her. "You see, she thought at first I was Frederick's newest girlfriend. She figured out years ago all the diamonds and furs and cars were out of his guilt. She assumed every unattached woman was after Frederick, and she was checking me out after she saw me out there with the girls.

The night I saw them in Looneyville, Frederick left, supposedly to go to work. She came to my house to see if he was there, and Barney surprised her. It was her pistol Frederick used to start the fire that killed Tucker."

She paused to marshal the story in her mind.

"Barney surprised her in the woods while she was on her way back to her car, and she shot him. He was probably just being friendly. She buried him, but then had the bright idea of discouraging me by leaving Barney's body for me to find. She apologized for that, and for the shot at me, too. She was actually aiming for the middle of the dashboard."

Flak took a deep breath. "She also set fire to the house with the fuel sample Frederick left behind. She knew you and I were outside and well away from the house. However, unlike Frederick, she didn't know how explosive it was. She just tossed it through the bathroom window. She was lucky she didn't blow her own head off."

"So what happens to her?"

"Well, I'm still debating on that. She promised to rebuild the house with Frederick's insurance, and I'm tempted to just leave it at that."

"You're not going to put her up on charges?"

Flak got up and started pacing again. "Well, her bullet didn't actually kill Frederick, mine did. So the only killing she's actually guilty of is killing Barney. She's making reparations for what she did to the house, and I don't think she's a danger to anyone with Frederick gone."

Garvey folded his arms, sighed. "Don't you think a jury of her peers ought to decide that?"

"Well, that's just it." She stopped her pacing and put into words what she'd been thinking ever since her conversation with the penitent woman.

"Raylene was basically trying to stop me from hurting her family, and none of her actions were meant to kill me. But even here, in the middle of the Bible belt, if a jury hears she was pretty much doing what God told her to do, they're going to put her away in the booby hatch. And she's not crazy. Unlike Faith-Ann, who is loony as a June bug."

Garv shook his head. "I trust your judgment, absolutely, but I don't understand how they're different."

"I stopped in the chapel this morning at the hospital, picked up a Bible, and found the passage Faith-Ann was talking about. By her own set of rules, Faith-Ann is a murderer. You got a Bible?"

Garvey walked to the small bookcase and handed her a massive white book with a blue cross on the cover. "Family Bible," he said and retreated to his recliner.

Flak placed the Good Book on the coffee table and began paging through it. "Here it is. This is the part of Numbers 35 before the piece Faith-Ann cited to me. Verse 16, 'And if he smite him with an instrument of iron, so that he die, he is a murderer: the murderer shall surely be put to death.' Faith-Ann, by the rules she lives by, is a murderer."

Garvey slowly shook his head. "No jury in this part of Texas will put her to death."

"No," Flak said slowly, "They'll put her over at Rusk State Hospital, and she will never, ever get out."

"Going back to the story of the Barnes clan, what about the rest of them?"

"Ben was never in it—he was and is a jerk, but nothing like Tucker's caliber. Maggie told me she was headed back to Dallas, to her husband. Jenny's deciding whether to run the store or sell it. She's going to finish getting her head on straight and see if she can't get her kids back."

"And Curtis Lee?"

"Someday, I might tell him his letter started the whole thing. I didn't mention that part to the girls—there's nobody who's going to tell him but me. Or you?" She made it into a question.

"Keep me out of it." Garvey raised both hands in the air.

Flak shrugged. "Maybe after the divorce is final I'll let him know. Or maybe never."

Garvey sat back in his recliner, and Flak placed the Bible on the coffee table, grabbed a cushion, and curled up in her corner of the couch once more.

"And what about us?" The question had been lurking around Garvey's eyes for a long time, and she'd expected something like it ever since his shouted declaration of love. It seemed like it had been years ago, not merely a few weeks.

She ran a finger around and around the fabric pattern on the couch arm.

"I think I've been running around and getting shot at and shooting people so much I'm too tired to make sense. You know what's been running through my head ever since I woke up this afternoon?"

He shook his head.

"Do you remember the nursery rhyme for counting a baby's toes? Well, I'm the last little pig, Garv, and I'm going to bed."

She headed for the bathroom to get ready for bed, but as she walked past him, she could see him counting on his fingers and mouthing the words.

Just as she shut the door, she heard him say, "Well, Andy, you horrible, rotten, kitty cat, looks like you may just be here a while. Whee, whee, whee! She's home."

Flak grinned and picked up her toothbrush.

--- The End ---

Contents

Author's Note:

Much of THIS LITTLE PIG was written with the places I grew up in as the setting—but much of it has been changed or invented to suit the story. So, while Nacogdoches County and the city of Nacogdoches (pronounced Nak-uh-DOH-chez) actually exist, there is no "Boozer Street."

Looneyville also exists (swear) and is in the general area where I was raised. The people I created for this story, bear no resemblance to anyone, alive or dead.

And for all those people who try to figure out which of the author's main characters are based on themselves, I can tell you I am not the main character. Other than that, further deponent sayeth not.

I have to acknowledge in this space the man who read the story from start to finish, and said "publish it." He's now my husband, Corey Hannon. Although THIS LITTLE PIG was written long before I met him, or even dreamed of him, somehow I based Garvey on him. Still don't know how I did that.

Regards,
Lisa C Hannon
2015

2017 – Note: For the 2nd edition, I got rid of a big old typo.
    Lisa